"Okay Sask... Andreas sa... ...old you to act like a ...thful fiancée but that does not mean you have to pretend to be an innocent virgin who has never…"

Abruptly he stopped, frowning as he mulled over the unwanted suspicions that were striking him as he looked at Saskia's pale face.

He could have sworn just now, when he had held her in his arms and kissed her…touched her…that he was the first man to make her feel so… For a moment he examined what he was thinking and then firmly dismissed his suspicions.

There was no way she could be so inexperienced, no way at all.

GREEK TYCOONS

**They're the men who have everything—
except a bride....**

Wealth, power, charm—what else could a
heart-stoppingly handsome tycoon need?
In the GREEK TYCOONS miniseries you
have already been introduced to some
gorgeous Greek multimillionaires who are
in need of wives.

Now it's the turn of favorite Harlequin Presents®
author PENNY JORDAN
with her attention-grabbing romance
THE DEMETRIOS VIRGIN

This tycoon has met his match and he's decided
he *has* to have her...*whatever* that takes!

Penny Jordan

THE DEMETRIOS VIRGIN

GREEK TYCOONS

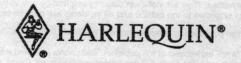

HARLEQUIN®

TORONTO • NEW YORK • LONDON
AMSTERDAM • PARIS • SYDNEY • HAMBURG
STOCKHOLM • ATHENS • TOKYO • MILAN • MADRID
PRAGUE • WARSAW • BUDAPEST • AUCKLAND

ISBN 0-373-12169-5

THE DEMETRIOS VIRGIN

First North American Publication 2001.

CHAPTER ONE

'FOUR forty-five.' Saskia grimaced as she hurried across the foyer of the office block where she worked, heading for the exit. She was already running late and didn't have time to pause when the receptionist called out. 'Sneaking off early... Lucky you!'

Andreas frowned as he heard the receptionist's comment. He was standing waiting for the executive lift and the woman who was leaving hadn't seen him, but he had seen her: a stunningly leggy brunette with just that gleam of red-gold in her dark locks that hinted at fieriness. He immediately checked the direction of his thoughts. The complication of a man to woman entanglement was the last thing he needed right now, and besides...

His frown deepened. Since he had managed to persuade his grandfather to semi-retire from the hotel chain which Andreas now ran, the older man had begun a relentless campaign to persuade and even coerce Andreas into marrying a second cousin. Such a marriage, in his grandfather's eyes, would unite not just the two branches of the family but the wealth of the family shipping line—inherited by his cousin—with that of the hotel chain.

Fortunately Andreas knew that at heart his grandfather was far more swayed by emotion than he liked to admit. After all, he had allowed his daughter, Andreas's mother, to marry an Englishman.

The somewhat clumsy attempts to promote a match between Andreas and his cousin Athena would merely afford Andreas some moments of wry amusement if it were not for one all-important fact—which was that Athena herself was even keener on the match than his grandfather. She had made her intentions, her *desires*, quite plain. Athena was a widow seven years his senior, with two children from her first marriage to another wealthy Greek, and Andreas suspected that it might have been Athena herself who had put the ridiculous idea of a marriage between them in his grandfather's head in the first place.

The lift had reached the penthouse floor and Andreas got out. This wasn't the time for him to be thinking about his personal affairs. *They* could wait. He was due to fly out to the Aegean island his grandfather owned, and where the family holidayed together, in less than a fortnight's time, but first his grandfather wanted a detailed report from him on his proposals to turn the flagging British hotel chain they had recently bought into as successful an enterprise as the rest of the hotels they owned.

Even though Andreas had become the company's chief executive, his grandfather still felt the need to challenge his business decisions. Still, the acquisition would ultimately be a good one—the chain-owned hotels were very run down and old fashioned, but had excellent locations.

Although officially he was not due to arrive at the chain's head office until tomorrow, Andreas had opted to do so this afternoon instead, and it looked as though he had just discovered one way at least in which profitability could be improved, he decided grimly, if all the staff were in the habit of 'sneaking off early', like the young woman he had just seen...

Sneaking off early! Saskia grimaced as she managed to hail a cruising taxi. If only! She had been at her desk for seven-thirty this morning, as she had been every morning for the last month, and neither had she had a lunch hour, but they had all been warned that Demetrios Hotels, who had taken over their own small chain, were relentless when it came to pruning costs. Tomorrow morning they were all due to meet their new boss for the first time, and Saskia wasn't exactly looking forward to the occasion. There had been a lot of talk about cutbacks and there had also been grapevine rumours about how very formidable Andreas Latimer was.

'The old man, his grandfather, had a reputation for running a tight ship, and if anything the grandson is even worse.'

'They both favour a "the guest is always right even when wrong" policy, and woe betide any employee who forgets it. Which is, of course, why their hotels are so popular...and so profitable,'

That had been the general gist of the gossip Saskia had heard.

Her taxi was drawing up outside the restaurant she had asked to be taken to. Hastily she delved into her handbag for her purse, paying the driver and then hurrying quickly inside.

'Oh, Saskia—*there* you are. We thought you weren't going to make it.'

'I'm sorry,' Saskia apologised to her best friend as she slipped into the spare seat at the table for three in the Italian restaurant where they had arranged to meet.

'There's been a panic on at work,' she explained. 'The new boss arrives tomorrow.' She pulled a face, wrinkling the elegant length of her dainty nose and screwing up her thick-lashed aquamarine eyes. She paused as she saw that her friend wasn't really listening, and that her normally happy, gentle face looked strained and unhappy.

'What's wrong?' she asked immediately.

'I was just telling Lorraine how upset I am,' Megan answered, indicating the third member of their trio, Megan's cousin Lorraine, an older woman with a brisk, businesslike expression and a slightly jaded air.

'Upset?' Saskia queried, a small frown marring the elegant oval of her face as she pushed her long hair back and reached hungrily for a bread roll. She was starving!

'It's Mark,' Megan said, her voice shaking a little and her brown eyes full of quiet despair.

'Mark?' Saskia repeated, putting down her roll so that she could concentrate on her friend. 'But I thought the two of you were about to announce your engagement.'

'Yes, we were...we are... At least, Mark wants to...' Megan began, and then stopped when Lorraine took over.

'Megan thinks he's involved with someone else...' she told Saskia grimly. 'Two-timing her.'

Older than Megan and Saskia by almost a decade,

and with a broken marriage behind her, Lorraine was inclined to be angrily contemptuous of the male sex.

'Oh, surely not, Megan,' Saskia protested. 'You told me yourself how much Mark loves you.'

'Well, yes, that's what I thought,' Megan agreed, 'Especially when he said that he wanted us to become engaged. But...he keeps getting these phone calls. And if I answer the phone whoever's ringing just hangs up. There've been three this week and when I ask him who it is he says it's just a wrong number.'

'Well, perhaps it is,' Saskia tried to reassure her, but Megan shook her head.

'No, it isn't. Mark keeps on hanging around by the phone, and last night he was talking on his mobile when I walked in and the moment he saw me he ended the call.'

'Have you *asked* him what's going on?' Saskia questioned her in concern.

'Yes. He says I'm just imagining it,' Megan told her unhappily.

'A classic male ploy,' Lorraine announced vigorously with grim satisfaction. 'My ex did everything to convince me that I was becoming paranoid and then what does he do? He moves in with his secretary, if you please!'

'I just wish that Mark would be honest with me,' Megan told Saskia, her eyes starting to fill with tears. 'If there *is* someone else...I... I just can't believe he's doing this... I thought he loved me...'

'I'm sure he does,' Saskia tried to comfort her. She had not as yet met her friend's new partner, but from what Megan had told her about him Saskia felt he sounded perfect for her.

'Well, there's one sure way to find out,' Lorraine announced. 'I read an article about it. There's this agency, and if you've got suspicions about your partner's fidelity you go to them and they send a girl to try to seduce him. That's what you should do,' she told Megan crisply.

'Oh, no, I couldn't,' Megan protested.

'You must,' Lorraine insisted forcefully. 'It's the only way you'll ever know whether or not you can trust him. I wish I'd been able to do something like that before I got married. You *must* do it,' she repeated. 'It's the only way you'll ever be sure. Mark is struggling to make ends meet since he started up his own business, Megan, and you've got that money you inherited from your great-aunt.'

Saskia's heart sank a little as she listened. Much as she loved her friend, she knew that Megan was inclined to allow herself to be dominated by her older and more worldly cousin. Saskia had nothing against Lorraine, indeed she liked her, but she knew from past experience that once Lorraine got the bit between her teeth there was no stopping her. She was fiercely determined to do things her own way, which Saskia suspected was at least part of the reason for the breakdown of her marriage. But right now, sympathetic though Saskia was to Megan's unhappiness, she was hungry...very hungry... She eyed the menu longingly.

'Well, it does *sound* a sensible idea,' Megan was agreeing. 'But I doubt there's an agency like that in Hilford.'

'Who needs an agency?' Lorraine responded. 'What *you* need is a stunningly gorgeous friend who Mark hasn't met and who can attempt to seduce him. If he responds...'

'A stunningly gorgeous friend?' Megan was musing. 'You mean like Saskia?'

Two pairs of female eyes studied Saskia whilst she gave in to her hunger and bit into her roll.

'Exactly,' Lorraine breathed fervently. 'Saskia would be perfect.'

'What?' Saskia almost choked on her bread. 'You *can't* be serious,' she protested. 'Oh, no, no way...' She objected when she saw the determination in Lorraine's eyes and the pleading in Megan's. 'No way at all.'

'Meg, this is crazy, you must see that,' she coaxed, trying to appeal to her friend's common sense and her conscience as she added winningly, 'How *could* you do something like that to Mark? You love him.'

'How can she risk committing herself to him unless she knows she can trust him?' Lorraine interjected sharply, adding emphatically, 'Good, that's settled. What we need to do now is to decide just where Saskia can accidentally run into Mark and put our plan into action.'

'Well, tonight is his boys' night out,' Megan ventured. 'And last night he said that they were planning to go to that new wine bar that's just opened. A friend of his knows the owner.'

'I can't do it,' Saskia protested. 'It...it's...it's immoral,' she added. She looked apologetically at Megan as she shook her head and told her, 'Meg, I'm sorry, but...'

'I should have thought you would *want* to help Megan, Saskia, to protect her happiness. Especially after all *she's* done for *you...*' Lorraine pointed out sharply.

Saskia worried guiltily at her bottom lip with her pretty white teeth. Lorraine was right. She *did* owe Megan a massive favour.

Six months ago, when they had been trying to fight off the Demetrios takeover bid, she had been working late every evening and at weekends as well. Her grandmother, who had brought her up following the breakdown of her young parents' marriage, had become seriously ill with a viral infection and Megan, who was a nurse, had given up her spare time and some of her holiday entitlement to care for the old lady.

Saskia shuddered to think even now of the potentially dangerous outcome of her grandmother's illness if Megan hadn't been there to nurse her. It had been on Saskia's conscience ever since that she owed her friend a debt she could never repay. Saskia adored her grandmother, who had provided her with a loving and stable home background when she had needed it the most. Her mother, who had given birth to Saskia at seventeen was a distant figure in her life, and her father, her grandmother's son, had become a remote stranger to both of them, living as he now did in China, with his second wife and young family.

'I know you don't approve, Saskia,' Megan was saying quietly to her, 'but I *have* to know that I can trust Mark.' Her soft eyes filled with tears. 'He means *so* much to me. He's everything I've *ever* wanted in a man. But...he dated so many girls before he met me, before he moved here, when he lived in London.' She paused. 'He swears that none of them ever meant anything serious to him and that he loves me.'

Privately Saskia wasn't sure that she could even begin to think about committing herself to a relationship with a man without being able to trust him—and trust him to such an extent that there would be no need for her to use any underhand methods to test his fidelity. But then she acknowledged that she was perhaps a trifle more wary of love than her friend. After all, her parents had believed themselves to be in love when they had run away to get married and conceived her, but within two years of doing so they had parted, leaving her grandmother with the responsibility of bringing her up.

Her grandmother! Now, as she looked at Meg's tearstained face, she knew she had no option but to go along with Lorraine's scheme.

'All right,' she agreed fatalistically. 'I'll do it.'

After Megan had finished thanking her she told her wryly, 'You'll have to describe your Mark to me, Megan, otherwise I shan't be able to recognise him.'

'Oh, yes, you will,' Megan said fervently with a small ecstatic sigh. 'He'll be the best-looking man there. He's gorgeous, Saskia...fantastically good-looking, with thick dark hair and the most sexy mouth you've ever seen. Oh, and he'll be wearing a blue shirt—to match his eyes. He always does. I bought them for him.'

'What time is he likely to get there?' Saskia asked Megan practically, instead of voicing her feelings.

'My car's in the garage at the moment, and since Gran's house is quite a way out of town...'

'Don't worry about that. I'll drive you there,' Lorraine volunteered, much to Saskia's surprise. Lorraine wasn't known to be over-generous—with anything!

'Yes, and Lorraine will pick you up later and take you home. Won't you, Lorraine?' Megan insisted with unexpected firmness. 'There's no taxi rank close to the wine bar and you don't want to be waiting for a mini-cab.'

A waiter was hovering, waiting to take their order, but bossily Lorraine shook her head, telling Megan and Saskia firmly, 'There won't be time for us to eat now. Saskia will have to get home and get ready. What time *is* Mark likely to go to the wine bar Megan?' she asked her cousin.

'About eight-thirty, I should think,' Megan answered.

'Right, then you need to get there for nine, Saskia,' Lorraine informed her, 'So I'll pick you up at half-eight.'

Two hours later Saskia was just coming downstairs when she heard the front doorbell. Her grandmother was away, spending several weeks with her sister in Bath. A little nervously Saskia smoothed down the skirt of her black suit and went to open the door.

Only Lorraine was standing outside. They had agreed that it would be silly to take the risk of Megan being seen and recognised. Now, as Lorraine studied her, Saskia could see the older woman beginning to frown.

'You'll have to wear something else,' she told Saskia sharply. 'You look far too businesslike and unapproachable in that suit. Mark's got to think you're approachable—remember. And I really think you ought to wear a different lipstick...red, perhaps, and more eye make-up. Look, if you don't believe me then read this.' Lorraine thrust an open magazine beneath Saskia's nose.

Reluctantly Saskia skimmed through the article, a small frown pleating her forehead as she read of the lengths the agency was prepared to have its girls go to in order to test the faithfulness of its clients' men.

'I can't do any of this,' she told Lorraine firmly. 'And as for my suit...'

Stepping into the hall and closing the front door behind her, Lorraine stood squarely in front of Saskia and told her vehemently, 'You have to—for Megan's sake. Can't you see what's happening to her, the danger she's in? She's totally besotted with this man; she's barely known him four months and already she's talking about handing over the whole of her inheritance to him...marrying him...having children with him. Do you know how much her great-aunt left her?' she added grimly.

Silently Saskia shook her head. She knew how surprised and shocked Megan had been when she had learned that she was the sole beneficiary under her great-aunt's will, but tactfully she had not asked her friend just how much money was involved.

Lorraine, it seemed, had not had similar qualms.

'Megan inherited nearly three million pounds,' she told Saskia, nodding her head in grim pleasure as she saw Saskia's expression.

'*Now* do you see how important it is that we do everything we can to protect her? I've tried to warn her umpteen times that her precious Mark might not be all he tries to make out he is, but she just won't listen. Now, thank goodness, she's caught him out and he's showing his true colours. For her sake, Saskia, you just do everything you can to prove how unworthy he is. Just imagine what it would do to her if he not only broke her heart but stole all her money as well. She'd be left with nothing.'

Saskia could imagine it all too well. Her grandmother had only a small pension to live on and Saskia, mindful of the sacrifices her grandmother had made when she was growing up, to make sure she did not go without the treats enjoyed by her peers, contributed as much as she could financially to their small household.

The thought of losing her financial independence and the sense of security that earning money of her own gave her was one that was both abhorrent and frightening to her, and Lorraine's revelations suddenly gave her not just the impetus but a real desire to do everything she could to protect her friend.

Megan, dear sweet trusting Megan, who still worked as a nurse despite her inheritance, deserved to find a man, a partner, who was truly worthy of her. And if this Mark wasn't... Well, perhaps then it would be for the best if her friend found out sooner rather than later.

'Perhaps if you took off the jacket of your suit,' Lorraine was saying now. 'You must have some kind of sexy summer top you could wear...or even just...'

She stopped as she saw Saskia's expression.

'Summer top, yes,' Saskia agreed. 'Sexy...no!'

As she saw the look on Lorraine's face Saskia suppressed a small sigh. It was pointless trying to explain to a woman like Lorraine that when nature had given one the kind of assets it had given Saskia, one learned very young that they could be something of a double-edged sword. To put it more bluntly, men—in Saskia's experience—did not need the double overload of seeing her body clad in 'sexy' clothes to encourage them to look twice at her. And in most cases to want to do much more than merely look!

'You must have *something*,' Lorraine urged, refusing to be defeated. 'A cardigan. You must have a cardigan—you could wear it sort of unbuttoned...'

'A cardigan? Yes, I have a cardigan,' Saskia agreed. She had bought it halfway through their cold spring when they had been on an economy drive at work and the heating had been turned off. But as for wearing it unbuttoned...!

'And red lipstick,' Lorraine was insisting, 'and more eye make-up. You'll have to let him know that you find him attractive...' She paused as Saskia lifted her eyebrows. 'It's for Megan's sake.'

In the end it was almost nine o'clock before they left the house, due to Lorraine's insistence that Saskia had to reapply her make-up with a far heavier hand than she would normally have used.

Uncomfortably Saskia refused to look at her reflection in the hall mirror. All that lipstick! It felt sticky, gooey, and as Lorraine drove her towards Hilford she had to force herself to resist the temptation to wipe it off. As for the unbuttoned cardigan she was wearing beneath her suit jacket—well, the moment she was inside the wine bar and out of Lorraine's sight she was going to refasten every single one of the top three buttons Lorraine had demanded that she left undone. True, they did nothing more than merely hint at a cleavage, but even that was far more of a provocation than Saskia would normally have allowed.

'We're here,' Lorraine announced as she pulled up outside the wine bar. 'I'll pick you up at eleven—that should give you plenty of time. Remember,' Lorraine hissed determinedly as Saskia got out of the car, 'We're doing this for Megan.'

We? But before Saskia could say anything Lorraine was driving off.

A man walking in the opposite direction paused on the pavement to give her an admiring glance. Automatically Saskia distanced herself from him and turned away, mentally squaring her shoulders as she headed for the entrance to the wine bar.

Lorraine had given her a long list of instructions, most of which had made Saskia cringe inwardly, and already her courage was beginning to desert her. There was no way she could go in there and pout and flirt in the enticing way that Lorraine had informed her she had to do. But if she didn't poor Megan could end up having her heart broken and her inheritance cheated away from her.

Taking a deep breath, Saskia pulled open the wine bar door.

CHAPTER TWO

ANDREAS saw Saskia the moment she walked in. He was seated at the bar, which was now being besieged by a crowd of young men who had come in just ahead of her. He could have stayed in and eaten in the office block's penthouse apartment—or even driven to the closest of their new acquisitions—but he had already endured two lengthy phone calls he would rather not have had this evening: one from his grandfather and another from Athena. So he had decided to go somewhere where neither of them could get in touch with him, having deliberately 'forgotten' to bring his mobile with him.

He hadn't been in a particularly good mood when he had arrived at the wine bar. Such places were not to his taste.

He liked good food served in comfortable surroundings where one could talk and think with ease, and there was also enough Greek in him for him to prefer somewhere more family centred and less of an obvious trawling ground for members of the opposite sex.

Thinking of the opposite sex made his mouth harden. Athena was becoming more and more brazen in her attempts to convince him that they should be together. He had been fifteen the first time he had been exposed to Athena's sexual aggression, and she had been twenty-two and about to be married.

He frowned as he watched Saskia. She was standing just inside the doorway, studying the room as though she was looking for someone. She turned her head and the light fell on her smoothly glossed lips.

Andreas sucked in his breath as he fought to control his unwanted reaction to her. What the hell was he doing? She was so damned obvious with that almost but not quite scarlet lipstick that he ought to be laughing, not... Not what? he asked himself caustically. Not wanting...lusting...

A strong surge of self-disgust lashed him. He had recognised her, of course. It was the girl from this afternoon, the one the receptionist had congratulated on her early departure from work. Then she had been wearing a minimum of make-up. Now... He eyed her lipsticked mouth and kohl-enhanced eyes grimly. She was wearing a suit with a short skirt...a very short skirt, he observed as she moved and he caught sight of the length of her sheer black tights-clad legs. A very, very short skirt!

As the turned-over waistband of her once respectably knee-length skirt made its presence felt, Saskia grimaced. Once she had found Mark she fully intended to make her way to the cloakroom and return her skirt to its normal length. It had been Lorraine, of course, who had insisted on shortening it.

'I can't go out like *that*,' Saskia had yelped.

'Don't be ridiculous,' Lorraine had derided her. 'That's nothing. Haven't you seen pictures from the sixties?'

'That was then,' Saskia had informed her firmly without letting her finish, but Lorraine had refused to give in and in the end Saskia had shrugged her

shoulders and comforted herself with the knowledge
that once Lorraine was out of sight she could do what
she liked with her skirt. The cardigan too was making
her feel uncomfortable, and unwittingly she started
to toy with the first of its unfastened buttons.

As he watched her Andreas's eyes narrowed. God,
but she was obvious, drawing attention to her breasts
like that... And what breasts! Andreas discovered
that he was starting to grind his teeth and, more importantly, that he was totally unable to take his eyes
off Saskia...

Sensing that she was being watched, Saskia turned
round and then froze as her searching gaze clashed
head-on with Andreas's hard-eyed stare.

For a breath of time Saskia was totally dazed, such
was the effect of Andreas's raw masculinity on her.
Her heart was pounding, her mouth dry, her body...
Helplessly transfixed, she fought desperately against
what she was feeling—against what she was not allowed to feel. For this was Megan's Mark—it had to
be. She could not really be experiencing what her
emotions were telling her she was experiencing, she
denied in panic. Not a woman like her, and not for
this man, Megan's man!

No other man in the place came anywhere near
matching the description Megan had given her as
closely as this one did. Mentally she ticked off
Megan's euphoric description of him—one Saskia
had previously put down to the near ravings of a
woman besottedly in love. Gorgeous, fantastically
good-looking, sexy... Oh, and he would be wearing
a blue shirt, Megan had told her, to match his eyes.
Well, Saskia couldn't make out the colour of his eyes

across the dimly lit distance that separated them, but she could certainly see that Megan had been right on every other count and her heart sank. So this was Megan's Mark. No wonder she was worrying so anxiously that he might be being unfaithful to her... A man who looked like this one did would have women pursuing him in droves.

Funny, but Megan hadn't mentioned the most important thing of all about him, which wasn't just that he was so spectacularly and sexually male but that he emanated a profound and intense air of authority that bordered almost on arrogance; it had struck Saskia the moment she had looked at him. That and the look of discreet male inspection quickly followed by a reactive resultant look of contemptuous disapproval.

That look... How *dare* he look at her like that? Suddenly all the doubts she had been harbouring about what she had agreed to do were vanquished.

Lorraine was right to be suspicious of such a man's motives, especially where a naïve, gentle, unworldly girl like Megan was concerned. Saskia didn't trust him one little bit. Megan needed a man who would appreciate her gentleness and treat her correspondingly. This man was powerful, daunting, awesome—and looking at him was, as Saskia was beginning to discover, something of a physical compulsion. She couldn't take her eyes off him. But that was just because she disliked him so much, she assured herself quickly, because she was so intensely aware of how very right Lorraine had been to want to test his loyalty to Megan.

Determinedly quelling the butterflies fluttering in

her stomach, Saskia took a deep breath, mentally reminding herself of what she had read in the article Lorraine had thrust under her nose. Then she had been horrified, repulsed by the lengths the girls hired by the agency were prepared to go to in order to entice and entrap their quarry into self-betrayal. It had even crossed her mind that no mere man could possibly find the strength to resist the kind of deliberate temptation those girls offered—everything from the most intense type of verbal flattery right up to outright offers of sex itself, although thankfully offers had been all they were.

A man like this one, though, must be used to women—attractive women—throwing themselves at him. 'He dated so many girls before he met me,' Megan had said innocently.

Saskia would just bet that he had. Megan was a honey, and Saskia loved her with a fierce loyalty, but even she had to admit that her friend did not possess the kind of glamorous instant eye appeal she suspected a man like this one would look for. But perhaps that was what he loved about her—the fact that she was so shy and homely. If he loved her... Well, that was up to Saskia to prove...or disprove...wasn't it?

With the light of battle shining in her eyes, Saskia made her way towards him.

Andreas watched her progress with a mixture of curiosity and disappointment. She was heading for him. He knew that, but the cool hauteur with which she not only ignored the interested looks she was collecting from other men as she did so but almost seemed not to notice them, was every bit as contrived as the unfastened buttons of the top she was wearing. It had to be! Andreas knew the type. He should do. After all, Athena...

'Oh, I'm sorry,' Saskia apologised as she reached Andreas's side and 'accidentally' stumbled against him. Straightening up, she stood next to him at the bar, giving him a winsomely apologetic smile as she moved so close to him that he could smell her scent... Not her perfume, which was light and floral, unexpectedly, but her *scent*, ...the soft, honey-sweet headily sensual and erotic scent that was her. And like a fool he was actually breathing it in, getting almost drunk on it...letting his senses react to it...to her...

Lorraine had coached her on her best approach and Saskia had memorised it, grimacing with loathing and distaste as she did so.

Andreas forced himself to step back from her and put some distance between them, but the bar was crowded and it was impossible for him to move away altogether, so instead he asked her coldly, 'I'm sorry...do I know you?'

His voice and demeanour were, he knew, cutting enough to make it plain that he knew what she was up to. Although why on earth a woman who looked like this one needed to trawl bars looking for men to pick up he had no idea. Or rather he did, but he preferred not to examine it too closely. There were women, as he already knew to his cost, who would do anything for money...anything...with anyone...

But Saskia was facing him now, her lipstick-glossed mouth parting in a smile he could see was forced as she purred, 'Er, no, actually, you don't...but I'm hoping that soon you will.'

Saskia was relieved that the bar was so dimly lit. She could feel the heat of her burning face. She had *never* in her most private thoughts even contemplated coming on to a man like this, never mind envisaged that she might actually do so. Quickly she hurried on to the next part of her prepared speech, parting her lips in what she hoped was a temptingly provocative smile whilst carefully running her tongue-tip over them.

Yuck! But all that lipstick felt repulsive.

'Aren't you going to ask me if I'd like a drink?' she invited coyly, batting her eyelashes in what she hoped was an appropriately enticing manner. 'I love the colour of your shirt,' she added huskily as she leaned closer. 'It matches your eyes...'

'If you think that you must be colour blind; my eyes are grey,' Andreas told her tersely. She was beginning to make him feel very angry. Her obviousness was nothing short of contemptible. But nothing like as contemptible as his own ridiculous reaction to her. What was he? A boy of eighteen? He was supposed to be a man...a mature, sophisticated, experienced, worldly man of thirty-odd—and yet here he was, reacting, *responding*, to the pathetically tired and jaded sexual tricks she was playing on him as eagerly as though... As though what? As though there was nothing he wanted to do right now more than take her to bed, to feel the hot urgency of her body beneath his, to hear her cry out his name through lips swollen with the mutual passion of their shared kisses whilst he...

'Look,' he told her sharply, cutting off the supply of lifeblood to his unwanted fantasies by the simple act of refusing to allow himself to think about them, 'you're making a big mistake.'

'Oh, no,' Saskia protested anxiously as he started to turn away from her. By rights she should simply accept what he was saying and go back to Megan and tell her that her beloved Mark was everything he was supposed to be. But an instinct she couldn't analyse was telling her that despite all the evidence to the contrary he was tempted. *Any* man could be tempted, she tried to tell herself fairly, but something inside her refused to allow her to listen.

'*You* could never be a mistake,' she purred suggestively. 'To any woman...'

Fatuously Andreas wondered if he had gone completely mad. To even think of desiring a woman who was openly propositioning him was anathema to everything he believed in. How could he possibly be even remotely attracted to her? He wasn't, of course. It was impossible. And as for that sudden inexplicable urge he had had to take her home with him, where she would be safe from the kind of attention her make-up and behaviour were bound to attract. Well, now he knew he *must* be seriously losing it.

If there was one thing he despised it was women like this one. Not that he preferred them to be demure or virginal. No. What he found most attractive was a woman who was proud to be herself and who expected his sex to respect her right to be what she was. The kind of woman who would automatically eschew any act that involved her presenting herself as some kind of sexual plaything and who would just as determinedly turn her back on any man who wanted her to behave that way. This woman...

'I'm sorry,' he told her, making it verbally plain that he was no such thing by the cold tone of his voice, 'but you're wasting your time. And time, as I can see,' he continued in a deceptively gentle voice, 'has to be money for a woman like you. So why don't you go away and find someone else who will be... er...more receptive to what you've got on offer than I am?'

White-faced, Saskia watched as he turned away from her and thrust his way towards the door. He had rejected her...refused her. He had... He had... Painfully she swallowed. He had proved that he was faithful to Megan and he had... He had looked at her as though...as though... Like a little girl, Saskia wiped the back of her hand across her lipsticked mouth, grimacing as she saw the stain the high-coloured gloss had left there.

'Hi there, gorgeous. Can I buy you a drink?'

Numbly she shook her head, ignoring the sour look the man who had approached was giving her as she stared at the door. There was no sign of Megan's man. He had gone—and she was glad. Of course she was. How could she not be? And she would be delighted to be able to report to Megan and Lorraine that Mark had not succumbed to her.

She glanced at her watch, her heart sinking. She still had over an hour to go before she met Lorraine. There was no way she could stay here in the bar on her own, attracting attention. Quickly she headed for the ladies. There was something she had to do.

In the cloakroom she fastened her cardigan and

wiped her face clean of the last of the red lipstick and the kohl eye-liner, replacing them both with her normal choice of make-up—a discreet application of taupe eye-shadow and a soft berry-coloured lipstick—and coiling up her long hair into a neat chignon. Then she waited in the ladies' room until an inspection of her watch told her she could finally leave.

This time as she made her way through the crowded bar it was a very different type of look that Saskia collected from the men who watched her admiringly.

To her relief Lorraine was parked outside, waiting for her.

'Well?' she demanded eagerly as Saskia opened the car door and got in.

'Nothing,' Saskia told her, shaking her head. 'He turned me down flat.'

'What?'

'Lorraine, careful…' Saskia cried out warningly as the other woman almost backed into the car behind her in shock.

'You mustn't have tried hard enough,' Lorraine told her bossily.

'I can assure you that I tried as hard as anyone could,' Saskia corrected her wryly.

'Did he *mention* Megan…tell you that he was spoken for?' Lorraine questioned her.

'No!' Saskia shook her head. 'But I promise you he made it plain that he wasn't interested. He looked at me…' She stopped and swallowed, unwilling to think about, never mind tell anyone else, just how Megan's beloved had looked at her. For some odd reason she refused to define just to remember the icy contempt she had seen in his eyes made her tremble between anger and pain.

'Where *is* Megan?' she asked Lorraine.

'She was called in unexpectedly to work an extra shift. She rang to let me know and I said we'd drive straight over to her place and meet up with her there.'

Saskia smiled wanly. By rights she knew she ought to be feeling far happier than she actually was. Though out of the three of them she suspected that Megan would be the only one who would actually be pleased to learn that her Mark had determinedly refused to be tempted.

Her Mark. *Megan's* Mark. There was a bitter taste in Saskia's mouth and her heart felt like a heavy lump of lead inside her chest.

What on earth was the matter with her? She couldn't possibly be jealous of Megan, could she? No! She couldn't be...she *must* not be!

'Are you sure you tried hard enough?' Lorraine was asking her sternly.

'I said everything you told me to say,' Saskia told her truthfully.

'And he didn't make any kind of response?'

Saskia could tell that Lorraine didn't believe her.

'Oh, he made a response,' she admitted grimly. 'It just wasn't the kind...' She stopped and then told her flatly, 'He wasn't interested, Lorraine. He must really love Megan.'

'Yes, if he prefers her to you he must,' Lorraine agreed bluntly. 'She's a dear, and I love her, but there's no way... You don't think he could have *guessed* what you were doing do you? No way he could have known...?'

'No, I don't,' Saskia denied. She was beginning to feel tired, almost aching with a sharp, painful need to be on her own. The last thing she wanted right now was to deal with someone like Lorraine, but she owed it to Megan to reassure her that she could trust Mark.

As they pulled up outside Megan's house Saskia saw that her car was parked outside. Her stomach muscles started to clench as she got out of Lorraine's car and walked up the garden path. Megan and Mark. Even their names sounded cosy together, redolent of domesticity...of marital comfort. And yet...if ever she'd met a man who was neither domesticated nor cosy it had been Megan's Mark. There had been an air of primitive raw maleness about him, an aura of power and sexuality, a sense that in his arms a woman could...*would*...touch such sensual heights of delight and pleasure that she would never be quite the same person again.

Saskia tensed. What on earth was she thinking? Mark belonged to Megan—her best friend, the friend to whom she owed her grandmother's life and good health.

Megan had obviously seen them arrive and was opening the door before they reached it, her face wreathed in smiles.

'It's all right,' Saskia told her hollowly. 'Mark didn't...'

'I know...I know...' Megan beamed as she ushered them inside. 'He came to see me at work and explained everything. Oh, I've been such an idiot...

Why on earth I didn't guess what he was planning I just don't know. We leave next week. He'd even told them at work what he was planning...that was the reason for all those calls. Plus the girl at the travel agency kept phoning. Oh, Saskia, I can't believe it. I've always longed to go to the Caribbean, and for Mark to have booked us such a wonderful holiday... The place we're going to specialises in holidays for couples. I'm so sorry you had a wasted evening. I tried to ring you but you'd already left. I thought you might have got here sooner. After all, once you'd realised that Mark wasn't at the wine bar...' She stopped as she saw the look on both her cousin's and Saskia's faces.

'What is it?' she asked them uncertainly.

'*You* said that you'd spoken to Mark,' Lorraine was saying tersely to Saskia.

'I did...' Saskia insisted. 'He was just as you described him to us, Megan...'

She stopped as Megan shook her head firmly.

'Mark wasn't there, Sas,' she repeated. 'He was with me at work. He arrived at half past eight and Sister gave me some time off so that we could talk. He'd guessed how upset I was and he'd decided that he would have to tell me what he was planning. He said he knew he couldn't have kept the secret for very much longer anyway,' she added fondly.

'And before you say a word,' she said firmly to her cousin, 'Mark is paying for everything himself.'

Saskia leaned weakly against the wall. If the man she had come on to hadn't been Megan's Mark, then just who on earth had he been? Her face became even paler. She had come on to a man she didn't know...a

total and complete stranger…a man who… She
swallowed nauseously, remembering the way she had
looked, the way she had behaved…the things she had
said. Thank God he was a stranger. Thank God she
would never have to see him again.

'Sas, you don't look well,' she could hear Megan
saying solicitously. 'What is it?'

'Nothing,' she fibbed, but Lorraine had already
guessed what she was thinking.

'Well, if the man in the wine bar wasn't Mark then
who on earth was he?' She demanded sharply.

'Who indeed?' Saskia echoed hollowly.

CHAPTER THREE

To SASKIA'S dismay she heard the town hall clock striking eight a.m. as she hurried to work. She had intended to be in extra early this morning but unfortunately she had overslept—a direct result of the previous evening's events and the fact that initially she had been mentally agonising so much over what she had done that she had been unable to get to sleep.

Officially she might not be due to be at her desk until nine a.m., but in this modern age that was not the way things worked, especially when one's hold on one's job was already dangerously precarious.

'There are bound to be cutbacks...redundancies,' the head of Saskia's department had warned them all, and Saskia, as she'd listened to him, had been sharply conscious that as the newest member of the team she was the one whose job was most in line to be cut back. It would be virtually impossible for her to get another job with the same kind of prospects in Hilford, and if she moved away to London that would mean her grandmother would be left on her own. At sixty-five her grandmother was not precisely old—far from it—and she had a large circle of friends, but the illness had left Saskia feeling afraid for her. Saskia felt she owed her such a huge debt, not only for bringing her up but for giving her so much love.

As she hurried into the foyer she asked Emma, the receptionist, anxiously, 'Has he arrived yet?'

There was no need to qualify who she meant by 'he', and Emma gave her a slightly superior smile as she replied, 'Actually he arrived yesterday. He's upstairs now,' she added smugly, 'interviewing everyone.' Her smugness and superiority gave way to a smile of pure feminine appreciation as she sighed. 'Just wait until you see him. He's gorgeous...with a great big capital G.'

She rolled her eyes expressively whilst Saskia gave her a wan smile.

She now had her own special and private—very private—blueprint of what a gorgeous man looked like, and she doubted that their new Greek boss came anywhere near to matching it.

'Typically, though, mind you,' the receptionist continued, oblivious to Saskia's desire to hurry to her office, 'he's already spoken for. Or at least he soon will be. I was talking to the receptionist at their group's head office and she told me that his grandfather wants him to marry his cousin. She's mega-wealthy and—'

'I'm sorry, Emma, but I must go,' Saskia interrupted her firmly. Office gossip, like office politics, was something Saskia had no wish to involve herself in, and besides... If their new boss was already interviewing people she didn't want to earn herself any black marks by not being at her desk when he sent for her.

Her office was on the third floor, an open plan space where she worked with five other people. Their boss had his own glass-walled section, but right now both it and the general office itself were empty.

Just as she was wondering what to do the outer door swung open and her boss, followed by the rest of her colleagues, came into the room.

'Ah, Saskia, there you are,' her boss greeted her.

'Yes. I had intended to be here earlier...' Saskia began, but Gordon Jarman was shaking his head.

'Don't explain now,' he told her sharply. 'You'd better get upstairs to the executive suite. Mr Latimer's secretary will be expecting you. Apparently he wants to interview everyone, both individually and with their co-department members, and he wasn't too pleased that you weren't here...'

Without allowing Saskia to say anything, Gordon turned on his heel and went into his office, leaving her with no option but to head for the lift. It was unlike Gordon to be so sharp. He was normally a very laid back sort of person. Saskia could feel the nervous feeling in her tummy increasing as she contemplated the kind of attitude Andreas Latimer must have adopted towards his new employees to cause such a reaction in her normally unflappable boss.

The executive suite was unfamiliar territory to Saskia. The only previous occasions on which she had entered it had been when she had gone for her initial interview and then, more recently, when the whole staff had been informed of the success of the Demetrios takeover bid.

A little uncertainly she got out of the lift and walked towards the door marked 'Personal Assistant to the Chief Executive'.

Madge Fielding, the previous owner's secretary,

had retired when the takeover bid's success had been announced, and when Saskia saw the elegantly groomed dark-haired woman seated behind Madge's desk she assumed that the new owner must have brought his PA with him from Demetrios head office.

Nervously Saskia gave her name, and started to explain that she worked for Gordon Jarman, but the PA waved her explanation aside, consulting a list in front of her instead and then saying coldly, without lifting her head from it, 'Saskia? Yes. You're late. Mr Latimer does not like… In fact I'm not sure…' She stopped and eyed Saskia with a disapproving frown. 'He may not have time to interview you now,' she warned, before picking up the phone and announcing in a very different tone of voice from the one she had used to address Saskia, 'Ms. Rodgers is here now, Andreas. Do you still want to see her?

'You *can* go in,' she informed Saskia. 'It's the door over there…'

Feeling like a naughty child, Saskia forced herself not to react, heading instead for the door the PA had indicated and knocking briefly on it before turning the handle and walking in.

As she stepped into the office the bright sunlight streaming in through the large windows momentarily dazzled her. All she could make out was the hazy outline of a man standing in front of the glass with his back to her, the brilliance of the sunlight making it impossible for her to see any more.

But Andreas could see Saskia. It hadn't surprised him that she should choose to arrive at work later than her colleagues; after all, he knew how she spent her evenings. What had surprised him had been the genuinely high esteem in which he had discovered she was held both by her immediate boss and her co-workers. It seemed that when it came to giving that extra metre, going that extra distance, Saskia was always the first to do so and the first to do whatever she could to help out her colleagues.

'Yes, it is perhaps unusual in a young graduate,' her boss had agreed when Andreas had questioned his praise of Saskia. 'But then she has been brought up by her grandmother and perhaps because of that her values and sense of obligation towards others are those of an older generation. As you can see from my report on her, her work is excellent and so are her qualifications.'

And she's a stunningly attractive young woman who seems to know how to use her undeniable 'assets' to her own advantage, Andreas had reflected inwardly, but Gordon Jarman had continued to enthuse about Saskia's dedication to her work, her kindness to her fellow employees, her ability to integrate herself into a team and work diligently at whatever task she was given, and her popularity with other members of the workforce.

After studying the progress reports her team leader and Gordon himself had made on her, and the photograph in her file, Andreas had been forced to concede that if he hadn't seen for himself last night the way Saskia could look and behave he would probably have accepted Gordon's glowing report at face value.

She was quite plainly a woman who knew how to handle his sex, even if with him she had made an error of judgement.

This morning, for instance, she had completely metamorphosed back into the dedicated young woman forging a career for herself—neatly suited, her hair elegantly sleeked back, her face free of all but the lightest touch of make-up. Andreas started to frown as his body suddenly and very urgently and unwontedly reminded him of the female allure of the body that was today concealed discreetly beneath a prim navy business suit.

Didn't he already have enough problems to contend with? Last night after returning from the wine bar he had received a telephone call from his mother, anxiously warning him that his grandfather was on the warpath.

'He had dinner with some of his old cronies last night and apparently they were all boasting about the deals they had recently pulled off. You know what they're like.' She had sighed. 'And your grandfather was told by one of them that he had high hopes of his son winning Athena's hand…'

'Good luck to him,' Andreas had told his mother uncompromisingly. 'I hope he does. That at least will get her and Grandfather off my back.'

'Well, yes,' his mother had agreed doubtfully. 'But at the moment it seems to have made him even more determined to promote a marriage between the two of you. And, of course, now that he's half retired he's got more time on his hands to plan and fret… It's such a pity that there isn't already someone in your life.' She had sighed again, adding with a chuckle, 'I honestly believe that the hope of a great-grandchild would thrill him so much that he'd quickly forget he'd ever wanted you to marry Athena!'

Someone else in his life? Had it really been exasperation and the headache he knew lay ahead of him with their new acquisition that had prompted him into making the rashest statement of his life in telling his mother, 'What makes you think there *isn't* someone?'

There had been a startled pause, just long enough for him to curse himself mentally but not for him to recall his impetuous words, before his mother had demanded in excitement, 'You mean there *is*? Oh, Andreas! Who? *When* are we going to meet her? Who is she? How did you...? Oh, darling, how wonderful. Your grandfather *will* be thrilled. Olympia, guess what...'

He had then heard her telling his sister.

He had tried to put a brake on their excitement, to warn them that he was only talking in 'ifs' and 'buts', but neither of them had been prepared to listen. Neither had his grandfather this morning, when he had rung at the ungodly hour of five o'clock to demand to know when he was to meet his grandson's fiancée.

Fiancée... How the hell his mother and sister had managed to translate an off the cuff remark made in irritation into a real live fiancée Andreas had no idea, but he did know that unless he produced this mythical creature he was going to be in very big trouble.

'You'll be bringing her to the island with you, of course,' his grandfather had announced, and his words had been a command and not a question.

What the hell was he going to do? He had eight

days in which to find a prospective fiancée and make it clear to her that their 'engagement' was nothing more than a convenient fiction. Eight days and she would have to be a good enough actress to fool not just his grandfather but his mother and sisters as well.

Irritably he moved out of the sunlight's direct beam, turning round so that Saskia saw him properly for the first time.

There was no opportunity for her to conceal her shock, or the soft winded gasp of dismay that escaped her discreetly glossed lips as her face paled and then flooded with burning hot colour.

'You!' she choked as she backed instinctively towards the door, her memories of the previous night flooding her brain and with them the sure knowledge that she was about to lose her job.

She certainly was an excellent actress, Andreas acknowledged as he observed her reaction—and in more ways than one. Her demeanour this morning was totally different from the way she had presented herself last night. But then no doubt she *was* horrified to discover that he was the man she had so blatantly propositioned. Even so, that look of sick dismay darkening her eyes and the way her soft bottom lip was trembling despite her attempts to stop it... Oh, yes, she was a first-rate actress—*a first-rate actress*!

Suddenly Andreas could see a welcome gleam of light at the end of the dark tunnel of his current problem. Oh, yes, indeed, a very definite beam of light.

'So Ms Rodgers.' Andreas began flaying into Saskia's already shredded self-confidence with all the delicacy of a surgeon expertly slicing through layer after layer of skin, muscle and bone. 'I have read the report Gordon Jarman has written on you and I must congratulate you. It seems that you've persuaded him to think very highly of you. That's quite an accomplishment for an employee so new and young. Especially one who adopts such an unconventional and, shall we say, elastic attitude towards time-keeping...leaving earlier than her colleagues in the evening and arriving later than them in the morning.'

'Leaving *early*?' Saskia stared at him, fighting to recover her composure. How had he known about *that*?

As though he had read her mind, he told her softly, 'I was in the foyer when you left...quite some time before your official finishing time.'

'But that was...' Saskia began indignantly.

However, Andreas did not allow her to finish, shaking his head and telling her coolly, 'No excuses, please. They might work on Gordon Jarman, but unfortunately for you they will not work with me. After all, I have seen how you comport yourself when you are not at work. Unless...' He frowned, his mouth hardening as he studied her with icy derision. 'Unless, of course, *that* is the reason he has given you such an unusually excellent report...'

'No!' Saskia denied straight away. 'No! I don't... Last night was a mistake,' she protested. 'I...'

'Yes, I'm afraid it was,' Andreas agreed, adding smoothly, 'For you at least. I appreciate that the salary you are paid is relatively small, but my grandfather would be extremely unhappy to learn that a member of our staff is having to boost her income in a way that can only reflect extremely badly on our company.' Giving her a thin smile he went on with deceptive amiability, 'How very fortunate for you that it wasn't in one of *our* hotels that you were...er... plying your trade and—'

'How dare you?' Saskia interrupted him furiously, her cheeks bright scarlet and her mouth a mutinous soft bow. Pride burned rebelliously in her eyes.

'How dare I? Rather I should say to you, how dare *you*,' Andreas contradicted her sharply, his earlier air of pleasantness instantly replaced by a hard look of contemptuous anger as he told her grimly, 'Apart from the unedifying moral implications of what you were doing, or rather attempting to do, has it ever occurred to you to consider the physical danger you could be putting yourself in? Women like you...'

He paused and changed tack, catching her off guard as he went on in a much gentler tone, 'I understand from your boss that you are very anxious to maintain your employment with us.'

'Yes. Yes, I am,' Saskia admitted huskily. There was no use denying what he was saying. She had already discussed her feelings and fears about the prospect of being made redundant with Gordon Jarman, and he had obviously recorded them and passed them on to Andreas. To deny them now would only convince him she was a liar—as well as everything else!

'Look... Please, I can explain about last night,' she told him desperately, pride giving way to panic. 'I know how it must have looked, but it wasn't... I didn't...' She stopped as she saw from his expression that he wasn't prepared even to listen to her, never mind believe her.

A part of her was forced to acknowledge that she

could hardly blame him...nor convince him either, unless she dragged Lorraine and Megan into his office to support her and she had far too much pride to do that. Besides, Megan wasn't capable of thinking of anything or anyone right now other than Mark and her upcoming Caribbean holiday, and as for Lorraine... Well, Saskia could guess how the older woman would revel in the situation Saskia now found herself in.

'A wise decision,' Andreas told her gently when she stopped speaking. 'You see, I despise a liar even more than I do a woman who...' Now it was his turn to stop, but Saskia knew what he was thinking.

Her face burned even more hotly, which made it disconcerting for her when he suddenly said abruptly, 'I've got a proposition I want to put to you.'

As she made a strangled sound of shock in her throat he steepled his fingers together and looked at her over them, like a sleek, well-fed predator watching a small piece of prey it was enjoying tormenting.

'What kind of proposition?' she asked him warily, but the heavy sledgehammer strokes of her heart against her ribs warned her that she probably already knew the answer—just as she knew why she was filled with such a shocking mixture of excitement and revulsion.

'Oh, not the kind you are probably most familiar with,' Andreas was telling her softly. 'I've read that some professional young women get a kick out of acting the part of harlots...'

'I was doing no such thing,' Saskia began heatedly, but he stopped her.

'I was there—remember?' he said sharply. 'If my

grandfather knew how you had behaved he would demand your instant dismissal.' His grandfather might have ceded most of the control of the business to Andreas, but Andreas could see from Saskia's expression that she still believed him.

'You don't *have* to tell him.' He could see the effort it cost her to swallow her pride and add a reluctant tremulous, 'Please...'

'I don't *have* to,' he agreed 'But whether or not I do depends on your response to my proposition.'

'That's blackmail,' Saskia protested.

'Almost as old a profession as the one you were engaging in last night,' Andreas agreed silkily.

Saskia began to panic. Against all the odds there was only one thing he could possibly want from her, unlikely though that was. After all, last night she had given him every reason to assume...to believe... But that had been when she had thought he was Mark, and if he would just allow her to explain...

Fear kicked through her, fuelling a panic that rushed her headlong into telling him aggressively, 'I'm surprised that a man like you needs to blackmail a woman into having sex with him. And there's no way that I...'

'Sex?' he questioned, completely astounding her by throwing back his head and laughing out loud. When he had stopped, he repeated, 'Sex?' adding disparagingly, 'With you? No way! It isn't *sex* I want from you,' he told her coolly.

'Not sex? Then...then what is it?' Saskia demanded shakily.

'What I want from you,' Andreas informed her

calmly, 'is your time and your agreement to pose as my fiancée.'

'What?' Saskia stared at him. 'You're mad,' she told him in disbelief.

'No, not mad,' Andreas corrected her sternly. 'But I am very determined not to be coerced into the marriage my grandfather wants to arrange for me. And, as my dear mother has so rightly reminded me, the best way to do that is to convince him that I am in love with someone else. That is the only way I can stop this ridiculous campaign of his.'

'You want *me*...to pose...as *your*...fiancée?' Saskia spaced the words out carefully, as though she wasn't sure she had heard them correctly, and then, when she saw the confirmation in his face, she denied fiercely, 'No. No way. No way at all!'

'No?' Andreas questioned with remarkable amiability. 'Then I'm afraid you leave me with no alternative but to inform you that there is a strong—a very strong possibility that we shall have to let you go as part of our regrettable but necessary cutbacks. I hope I make myself clear.'

'No! You can't do that...' Saskia began, and then stopped as she saw the cynical way he was looking at her.

She was wasting her time. There was no way he was even going to listen to her, never mind believe her. He didn't *want* to believe her. It didn't suit his plans to believe her...she could see that. And if she refused to accede to his commands then she knew that he was fully capable of carrying out his threat against her. Saskia swallowed. She was well and truly trapped, with no way whatsoever of escaping.

'Well?' Andreas mocked her. 'You still haven't given me your reply. Do you agree to my proposition, or...?'

Saskia swallowed the bitter taste of bile and defeat lodged in her throat. Her voice sounded raw, rasping...it hurt her to speak but she tried to hold up her head as she told him miserably, 'I agree.'

'Excellent. For form's sake I suggest that we invent a previously secret accidental meeting between us—perhaps when I visited Hilford prior to our takeover. Because of the negotiations for the takeover we have kept our relationship...our love for one another...a secret. But now...now there is no need for secrecy any more, and to prove it, and to celebrate our freedom today I shall take you out for lunch.'

He frowned and paused. 'We shall be flying out to the Aegean at the end of next week and there are things we shall be expected to know about one another's background!'

'Flying out to *where*?' Saskia gasped. 'No, I can't. My grandmother...'

Andreas had heard from Gordon Jarman that she lived with her grandmother, and now one eyebrow rose as he questioned silkily, 'You are engaged to me now, my beloved, surely *I* am of more importance than your grandmother? She will, I know, be surprised about our relationship, but I am sure she will appreciate just why we had to keep our love for one another to ourselves. If you wish I am perfectly prepared to come with you when you explain...everything to her...'

'No!' Saskia denied in panic. 'There's no need anyway. She's in Bath at the moment, staying with her sister. She's going to be there for the next few weeks. You can't do this,' she told him in agitation. 'Your grandfather is bound to guess that we're not…that we don't… And…'

'But he must *not* be *allowed* to guess any such thing,' Andreas told her gently. 'You are an excellent actress, as I have already seen for myself, and I'm sure you will be able to find a way of convincing him that we *are* and we *do*, and should you feel that you do need some assistance to that end…' His eyes darkened and Saskia immediately took a step backwards, her face flaming with embarrassed colour as she saw the way he was looking at her.

'Very nice,' he told her softly, 'But perhaps it might not be wise to overdo the shy, virginal bit. My grandfather is no fool. I doubt that he will expect a man of my age to have fallen passionately in love with a woman who is not equally sexually aware. I am, after all, half-Greek, and passion is very much a factor of the male Greek personality and psyche.'

Saskia wanted to turn and run away. The situation was becoming worse by the minute. What, she wondered fatalistically, would Andreas do if he ever learned that she was not 'sexually aware', as he had termed it, and that in fact her only experience of sex and passion was limited to a few chaste kisses and fumbled embraces? She had her parents to thank for her caution as a teenager where sexual experimentation had been concerned, of course. Their rash behaviour had led to her dreading that she might repeat their foolishness. But there was, of course, no way that Andreas could ever know that!

'It's now almost ten,' Andreas informed her

briskly, looking at his watch. 'I suggest you go back to your office and at one p.m. I'll come down for you and take you out to lunch. The sooner we make our relationship public now, the better.'

As he spoke he was moving towards her. Immediately Saskia started to panic, gasping out loud in shock as the door opened to admit his PA in the same heartbeat as Andreas reached out and manacled Saskia's fragile wrist-bone in the firm grip of his fingers and thumb.

His skin was dark, tanned, but not so much so that one would automatically guess at his Greek blood, Saskia recognised. His eyes *were* grey, she now saw, and not blue as she had so blush-makingly suggested last night, and they added to the confusion as to what nationality he might be, whilst his hair, though very, very dark, was thick and straight. There was, though, some whisper of his ancient lineage in his high cheekbones, classically sculptured jaw and aquiline nose. They definitely belonged to some arrogant, aristocratic ancient Greek nobleman, and he would, she suspected, be very much inclined to dominate those around him, to stamp his authority on everything he did—and everyone he met.

'Oh, Andreas,' the PA was exclaiming, looking in flustered disbelief at the way her boss was drawing Saskia closer to him, 'I'm sorry to interrupt you but your grandfather has been on—twice!'

'I shall ring my grandfather back shortly,' Andreas responded smoothly, adding equally smoothly, 'Oh, and I don't want any appointments or any interruptions from one to two-thirty today. I shall be taking my fiancée to lunch.'

As he spoke he turned to Saskia and gave her such a look of melting tender sensuality, so completely redolent of an impatient lover barely able to control his desire for her, that for a breath of time she was almost taken in herself. She could only stare back at him as though she had been hypnotised. If he had given her a look like that last night... Stop it, she warned herself immediately, shaken by the unexpected thought.

But if his behaviour was shocking her it was shocking his PA even more, she recognised as the other woman gave a small choked gurgle and then shook her head when Andreas asked her urbanely if anything was wrong.

'No. I was just... That is... No...not at all...'

'Good. Oh, and one more thing. I want you to book an extra seat on my flight to Athens next week. Next to mine...for Saskia...' Turning away from his PA he told Saskia huskily, 'I can't wait to introduce you to my family, especially my grandfather. But first...'

Before Saskia could guess what he intended to do he lifted her hand to his mouth, palm facing upwards. As she felt the warmth of his breath skimming her skin Saskia started to tremble, her breath coming in quick, short bursts. She felt dizzy, breathless, filled with a mixture of elation, excitement and shock, a sense of somehow having stepped outside herself and become another person, entered another life—a life that was far more exciting than her own, a life that could lead to the kind of dangerous, magical, awe-inspiring experiences that she had previously thought could never be hers.

Giddily she could hear Andreas telling her huskily, 'First, my darling, we must find something pretty to adorn this bare finger of yours. My grandfather would not approve if I took you home without a ring that states very clearly my intentions.'

Saskia could hear quite plainly the PA's sudden shocked indrawn breath, but once again the other woman could not be any more shocked than she was herself. Andreas had claimed that she was a good actress, but he was no slouch in that department himself. The look that he was giving her right now alone, never mind the things he had said...

After his PA had scuttled out of his office, closing the door behind her, she told him shakily, 'You do realise, don't you, that by lunchtime it will be all over the office?'

'All over the office?' he repeated, giving her a desirous look. 'My dear, I shall be very surprised and even more disappointed if our news has not travelled a good deal further than that.'

When she gave him an uncomprehending look he explained briefly, 'By lunchtime I fully expect it to have travelled at least as far as Athens...'

'To your grandfather,' Saskia guessed.

'Amongst others,' Andreas agreed coolly, without enlightening her as to who such 'others' might be.

Unexpectedly there were suddenly dozens of questions she wanted to ask him: about his family, as well as his grandfather, and the island he intended to take her to, and about the woman his grandfather wanted him to marry. She had a vague idea that Greeks were very interested in protecting family interests and according to Emma his cousin was 'mega wealthy', as was Andreas himself.

Somehow, without knowing quite how it had happened, she discovered that Andreas had released her hand and that she was walking through the door he had opened for her.

'Ready, Saskia?'

Saskia felt the embarrassed colour start to seep up under her skin as Andreas approached her desk. Her colleagues were studiously avoiding looking openly at them but Saskia knew perfectly well that they were the cynosure of their attention. How could they not be?

'Gordon, I'm afraid that Saskia is going to be late back from lunch,' Andreas was announcing to her bemused boss as he came out from his office.

'Have you told him our news yet, darling,' Andreas asked her lovingly.

'Er...no...' Saskia couldn't bring herself to look directly at him.

'Saskia,' she could hear her boss saying weakly as he looked on disbelievingly, 'I don't understand...'

He would understand even less if she tried to explain to him what was *really* happening, Saskia acknowledged bleakly. It seemed to her that it was a very unfair thing to do to deceive the man who had been so kind to her but what alternative did she really have.

'You mustn't blame Saskia,' Andreas was saying protectively. 'I'm afraid I'm the one who's at fault. I insisted that our relationship should be kept a secret until the outcome of our takeover bid became public.

I didn't want Saskia to be accused of having conflicting loyalties—and I must tell you, Gordon, that she insisted that any kind of discussion about the takeover was off-limits between us... Mind you, talking about work was not exactly *my* number one priority when we were together,' Andreas admitted, with a sensual look at Saskia that made her face burn even more hotly and caused more than one audible and envious gasp from her female co-workers.

'Why did you have to do *that*?' Saskia demanded fretfully the moment they were alone and out of earshot.

'Do what?' Andreas responded unhelpfully.

'You know perfectly well what I mean,' Saskia protested. 'Why couldn't we just have met somewhere?'

'In secret?' He looked more bored now than amorous, his eyebrows drawing together as he frowned impatiently down at her. He was a good deal taller than her, well over six foot, and it hurt her neck a little, craning to look up at him. She wished he wouldn't walk so close to her; it made her feel uncomfortable and on edge and somehow aware of herself as a woman in a way that wasn't familiar to her.

'Haven't I already made it plain to you that the whole object of this exercise is to bring our relationship into the public domain? Which is why—' He smiled grimly at Saskia as he broke off from what he was saying to tell her silkily, 'I've booked a table at the wine bar for lunch. I ate there last night and I have to say that the food was excellent—even if what happened later was less...palatable...'

Suddenly Saskia had had enough.

'Look, I keep trying to tell you, last night was a mistake. I…'

'I completely agree with you,' Andreas assured her. 'It *was* a mistake…*your* mistake…and whilst we're on the subject, let me warn you, Saskia, if you *ever* manifest anything similar whilst you are engaged to *me*, if you ever even *look* at another man…' He stopped as he saw the shock widening her eyes.

'I'm half-Greek, my dear,' he reminded her softly. 'And when it comes to *my* woman, I'm more Greek than I am British…very much more…'

'I'm *not* your woman,' was the only response Saskia found she could make.

'No,' he agreed cynically. 'You belong to any man who can afford you, don't you, in reality? But…' He stopped again as he heard the sharp sound of protest she made, her face white and then red as her emotions overwhelmed her self-control.

'You have no right to speak to me like that,' Saskia told him thickly.

'No right? But surely as your fiancée I have *every* right,' Andreas taunted her, and then, before she could stop him, he reached out and ran one long finger beneath her lower eyelashes, collecting on it the angry humiliated tears that had just fallen. 'Tears?' he mocked her. 'My dear, you are an even better actress then I thought.'

They had reached the wine bar and Saskia was forced to struggle to control her emotions as he opened the door and drew her inside.

'I don't want anything to eat. I'm not hungry,' she told him flatly once they had been shown to their table.

'Sulking?' he asked her succinctly. 'I can't force you to eat, but I certainly don't intend to deny *myself* the pleasure of enjoying a good meal.'

'There are things we have to discuss,' he added in a cool, businesslike voice as he picked up the menu she had ignored and read it. 'I know most of your personal details from your file, but if we are to convince my family and especially my grandfather that we are lovers, then there are other things I shall need to know...and things you will need to know about me.'

Lovers... Saskia just managed to stop herself from shuddering openly. If she had to accede to his blackmail then she was going to have to learn to play the game by his rules or risk being totally destroyed by him.

'Lovers.' She gave him a bleak smile. 'I thought Greek families didn't approve of sex before marriage.'

'Not for their *own* daughters,' he agreed blandly. 'But since you are *not* Greek, and since *I* am half-British I am sure that my grandfather will be more...tolerant...'

'But he wouldn't be tolerant if you were engaged to your cousin?' Saskia pressed, not sure why she was doing so and even less sure just why the thought of his cousin should arouse such a sensation of pain and hostility within her.

'Athena, my cousin, is a *widow*, a previously married woman, and naturally my grandfather...' He paused and then told her dryly, 'Besides, Athena herself would never accept my grandfather's interference in any aspect of her life. She is a very formidable woman.'

'She's a *widow*?' For some reason Saskia had assumed that this cousin was a young girl. It had never occurred to her that she might already have been married.

'A widow,' Andreas confirmed. 'With two teenage children.'

'Teenage!'

'She married at twenty-two,' Andreas told her with a shrug. 'That was almost twenty years ago.'

Saskia's eyes widened as she did her sums. Athena was obviously older than Andreas. A lonely and no doubt vulnerable woman who was being pressurised into a second marriage she perhaps did not want, Saskia decided sympathetically.

'However, you need not concern yourself too much with Athena, since it is doubtful that you will meet her. She lives a very peripatetic existence. She has homes in Athens, New York and Paris and spends much of her time travelling between them, as well as running the shipping line she inherited.'

A shipping line and a hotel chain. No wonder Andreas's grandfather was so anxious for them to marry. It amazed Saskia that Andreas was not equally keen on the match, especially knowing the hard bargain he had driven over the takeover.

As though he had guessed what she was thinking, he leaned towards her and told her grittily, 'Unlike you, *I* am not prepared to sell myself.'

'I was *not* selling myself,' Saskia denied hotly, and then frowned as the waiter approached their table carrying two plates of delicious-looking food.

'I didn't order a meal,' she began as he set one of them down in front of her and the other in front of Andreas.

'No. I ordered it for you,' Andreas told her. 'I don't like to see my women looking like skinny semi-starved rabbits. A Greek man may be permitted to beat his wife, but he would never stoop to starving her.'

'Beat...' Saskia began rising to the bait and then stopped as she saw the glint in his eyes and realised that he was teasing her.

'I suspect you are the kind of woman, Saskia, who would drive a saint, never mind a mere mortal man, to be driven to subdue you, to master you and then to wish that he had had the strength to master himself instead.'

Saskia shivered as the raw sensuality of what he was saying hit her like a jolt of powerful electricity. What was it about him that made her so acutely aware of him, so nervously on edge?

More to distract herself than anything else she started to eat, unaware of the ruefully amused look Andreas gave her as she did so. If he didn't know better he would have said that she was as inexperienced as a virgin. The merest allusion to anything sexual was enough to have her trembling with reaction, unable to meet his gaze. It was just as well that he knew it was all an act, otherwise... Otherwise what? Otherwise he might be savagely tempted to put his words into actions, to see if she trembled as deliciously when he touched her as she did when he spoke to her.

To counter what he was feeling he began to speak to her in a crisp, businesslike voice.

'There are certain things you will need to know about my family background if you are going to convince my grandfather that we are in love.'

He proceeded to give her a breakdown of his immediate family, adding a few cautionary comments about his grandfather's health.

'Which does not mean that he is not one hundred and fifty per cent on the ball. If anything, the fact that he is now prevented from working so much means that he is even more ferociously determined to interfere in my life than he was before. He tells my mother that he is afraid he will die before I give him any great-grandchildren. If that is not blackmail I don't know what is,' Andreas growled.

'It's obviously a family vice,' Saskia told him mock sweetly, earning herself a look that she refused to allow to make her quake in her shoes.

'Ultimately, of course, our engagement will have to be broken,' Andreas told her unnecessarily. 'No doubt our sojourn on the island will reveal certain aspects of our characters that we shall find mutually unappealing, and on our return to England we shall bring our engagement to an end. But at least I shall have bought myself some time...and hopefully Athena will have decided to accept one of the many suitors my grandfather says are only too willing to become her second husband.'

'And if she doesn't?' Saskia felt impelled to ask.

'*If* she doesn't, we shall just have to delay ending our engagement until either she does or I find an alternative way of convincing my grandfather that one of my sisters can provide him with his great-grandchildren.'

'You don't *ever* want to marry?' Saskia was startled into asking.

'Well, let's just say that since I have reached the age of thirty-five without meeting a woman who has made me feel my life is unliveable without her by my side, I somehow doubt that I am likely to do so now. Falling in love is a young man's extravagance. In a man past thirty it is more of a vain folly.'

'My father fell in love with my mother when he was seventeen,' Saskia couldn't stop herself from telling him. 'They ran away together...' Her eyes clouded. 'It was a mistake. They fell out of love with one another before I was born. An older man would at least have had some sense of responsibility towards the life he had helped to create. My father was still a child himself.'

'He abandoned you?' Andreas asked her, frowning.

'They both did,' Saskia told him tersely. 'If it hadn't been for my grandmother I would have ended up in a children's home.'

Soberly Andreas watched her. Was *that* why she went trawling bars for men? Was she searching for the male love she felt she had been denied by her father? His desire to exonerate her from her behaviour irritated him. *Why* was he trying to make excuses for her? Surely he hadn't actually been taken in by those tears earlier.

'It's time for us to leave,' he told her brusquely.

CHAPTER FOUR

IF SOMEONE had told her two weeks ago that she would be leaving behind her everything that was familiar to fly to an unknown Greek island in the company of an equally unknown man to whom she was supposed to be engaged Saskia would have shaken her head in denial and amusement—which just went to show!

Which just went to show what a combination of male arrogance, self-belief and determination could do, especially when it was allied to the kind of control that one particular male had over her, Saskia fretted darkly.

In less than fifteen minutes' time Andreas would be picking her up in his Mercedes for the first leg of their journey to Aphrodite, the island Andreas's grandfather had bought for his wife and named after the goddess of love.

'Theirs was a love match but one that had the approval of both families,' Andreas had told Saskia when he had been briefing her about his background.

A love match...unlike *their* bogus engagement. Just being a party to that kind of deceit, even though it was against her will, made Saskia feel uncomfortable, but nowhere near as uncomfortable as she had felt when she had had to telephone her grandmother and lie to her, saying that she was going away on business.

Andreas had tried to insist that she inform her grandmother of their engagement, but Saskia had refused.

'*You* may be happy to lie to your family about our supposed "relationship",' she had told him with a look of smoky-eyed despair. 'But I *can't* lie to my grandmother about something so...' She hadn't been able to go on, unwilling to betray herself by admitting to Andreas that her grandmother would never believe that Saskia had committed herself and her future to a man without loving him.

Once the fall-out from the news of her 'engagement' had subsided at work, her colleagues had treated her with both wary caution and distance. She was now the boss's fiancée and as such no longer really 'one of them'.

All in all Saskia had spent the week feeling increasingly isolated and frightened, but she was too proud to say anything to anyone—a hang-up, she suspected, from the days of her childhood, when the fact that her parents' story was so widely known, coupled with the way she had been dumped on her grandmother, had made her feel different, distanced from her schoolmates, who had all seemed to have proper mummies and daddies.

Not that anyone could have loved her more than her grandmother had done, as Saskia was the first to acknowledge now. Her home background had in reality been just as loving and stable, if not more so, than that of the majority of her peers.

She gave a small surreptitious look at her watch. Less than five minutes to go. Her heart thumped heavily. Her packed suitcase was ready and waiting in the hall. She had agonised over what she ought to take and in the end had compromised with a mixture of the summer holiday clothes she had bought three years previously, when she and Megan had gone to Portugal together, plus some of her lightweight office outfits.

She hadn't seen Andreas since he had taken her out for lunch—not that she had minded *that*! No indeed! He had been attending a gruelling schedule of business meetings—dealing, if the trickles of gossip that had filtered through the grapevine were anything to go by, heroically with the problems posed by the challenging situation the hotels had fallen into prior to the takeover.

'He's visited every single one of our hotels,' Saskia had heard from one admiring source. 'And he's been through every single aspect of the way they're being run—and guess what?'

Saskia, who had been on the edge of the group who'd been listening eagerly to this story, had swallowed uncomfortably, expecting to hear that Andreas had instituted a programme of mass sackings in order to halt the flood of unprofitable expenses, but to her astonishment instead she had heard, 'He's told everyone that their job is safe, provided they can meet the targets he's going to be setting. Everywhere he's been he's given the staff a pep talk, told them how much he values the acquisition his group has made and how he personally is going to be held responsible by the board of directors if he can't turn it into a profit-making asset.'

The gossip was that Andreas had a way with him that had his new employees not only swearing allegiance but apparently praising him to the skies as well.

Well, they obviously hadn't witnessed the side to his character she had done, was all that Saskia had been able to think as she listened a little bitterly to everyone's almost euphoric praise of him.

It was ten-thirty now, and he wasn't... Saskia tensed as she suddenly saw the large Mercedes pulling up outside her grandmother's house. Right on time! But of course Andreas would not waste a precious second of his time unless he had to, especially not on her!

By the time he had reached the front door she had opened it and was standing waiting for him, her suitcase in one hand and her door key in the other.

'What's that?'

She could see the way he was frowning as he looked down at her inexpensive case and immediately pride flared through her sharpening her own voice as she answered him with a curt, 'My suitcase.'

'Give it to me,' he instructed her briefly.

'I can carry it myself,' Saskia informed him grittily.

'I'm sure you can,' Andreas agreed, equally grimly. 'But...'

'But what?' Saskia challenged him angrily. 'But Greek men do not allow women to carry their own luggage nor to be independent from them in any way?'

Saskia could see from the way Andreas's mouth tightened that he did not like what she had said. For some perverse reason she felt driven to challenge him, even though a part of her shrank from the storm signals she could see flashing in his eyes.

'I'm afraid in this instance you should perhaps blame my English father rather than my Greek mother,' he told her icily. 'The English public school he insisted I was sent to believed in what is now considered to be an outdated code of good manners for its pupils.' He gave her a thin, unfriendly look. 'One word of warning to you. My grandfather is inclined to be old-fashioned about such things. He will not understand your modern insistence on politically correct behaviour, and whilst you are on the island…'

'I have to do as *you* tell me,' Saskia finished bitterly for him.

If this was a taste of what the next few weeks were going to be like she didn't know how she was going to survive them. Still, at least there would be one benefit of their obvious hostility to one another. No one who would be observing them together would be surprised when they decided to end their 'engagement'.

'Our flight leaves Heathrow at nine tomorrow morning, so we will need to leave the apartment early,' Andreas informed Saskia once they were in the car.

'The *apartment*?' Saskia questioned him warily immediately.

'Yes,' Andreas confirmed. 'I have an apartment in London. We shall be staying there tonight. This afternoon we shall spend shopping.'

'Shopping…?' Saskia began to interrupt, but Andreas overruled her.

'Yes, shopping,' he told her cautiously. 'You will need an engagement ring, and...' He paused and gave her a brief skimming look of assessment and dismissal that made her itch to demand that he stop the car immediately. Oh, how she would love to be able to tell him that she had changed her mind...that there was no way she was going to give in to his blackmail. But she knew there was no way she could.

'You will need more suitable clothes.'

'If you mean holiday clothes,' Saskia began, 'they are in my case, and...'

'No, I do not mean "holiday" clothes.' Andreas stopped her grimly. 'I am an independently wealthy man, Saskia; you don't need me to tell you that. Your department's investigations prior to our takeover must have informed you to the nearest hundred thousand pounds what my asset value is. My grandfather is a millionaire many times over, and my mother and my sisters are used to buying their clothes from the world's top designers, even though none of them are what could be considered to be fashion victims or shopaholics. Naturally, as my fiancée...'

Without allowing him to finish Saskia took a deep, angry breath and told him dangerously, 'If you think that I am going to let *you* buy my clothes...'

With only the briefest of pauses Andreas took control of the situation from her by asking smoothly, 'Why not? After all, you were prepared to let me buy your *body*. Me or indeed any other man who was prepared to pay for it.'

'No! That's not true,' Saskia denied with a shocked gasp.

'Very good,' Andreas mocked her. 'But you can

save the special effects for my family. I know *exactly* what you are—remember. Think of these clothes as a perk of your job.' He gave her a thin, unkind smile. 'However, having said that, I have to add that I shall want to vet whatever you wish to purchase. The image I want you to convey to my family as my fiancée is one of elegance and good taste.'

'What are you trying to suggest?' Saskia hissed furiously at him. 'That left to my own devices I might choose something more suited to a...?' She stopped, unable to bring herself to voice the words burning a painful brand in her thoughts.

To her bemusement, instead of saying them for her Andreas said coolly, 'You are obviously not used to buying expensive clothes and there is no way I want you indulging in some kind of idiotic unnecessary economy which would negate the whole purpose of the exercise. I don't want you buying clothes more suitable for a young woman on a modest salary than the fiancée of an extremely wealthy man,' he informed her bluntly, in case she had not understood him the first time.

For once Saskia could think of nothing to say, but inside she was a bundle of fury and shame. There was no way she could stop Andreas from carrying out his plans, she knew that, but she fully intended to keep a mental record of everything he spent so that ultimately she could repay him, even if doing so totally depleted the small nest egg she had been carefully saving.

'No more objections?' Andreas enquired smoothly. 'Good, because I promise you, Saskia, I mean to have my way—even if that entails dressing you and undressing you myself to get it. Make no mistake, when we arrive on Aphrodite you will be arriving as my fiancée.'

As he drove down the slipway onto the motorway and the powerful car picked up speed Saskia decided diplomatically that quarrelling with him whilst he was driving at such a speed would be very foolish indeed. It was over half an hour later before she recognised that, in her anxiety to reject Andreas's claimed right to decide what she should wear, she had neglected to deal with the more important issue of her discomfort at the idea of spending the night with him.

But what did she really have to fear? Certainly not any sexual advances from Andreas. He had, after all, made it shamingly plain what he thought of her sexual morals.

She had far too much pride to admit to him that she felt daunted and apprehensive at the thought of sharing the intimacy of an apartment with him. On the island it would be different. There they would be with his family and the staff who ran the large villa complex he said his grandfather had had built on it.

No, she would be wise to grit her teeth and say nothing rather than risk exposing herself to his disbelief and mocking contempt by expressing her anxieties.

As she waited for the chauffeur to load her luggage into the boot of her hired limousine Athena tapped one slender expensively shod foot impatiently.

The moment she had heard the news that Andreas was engaged and about to bring his fiancée to

Aphrodite on an official visit to meet his family she had sprung into action. Fortunately an engagement was not a marriage, and she certainly intended to make sure that *this* engagement never made it as far as a wedding.

She knew why Andreas had done it, of course. He was, after all, Greek to the very marrow of his bones—even if he chose to insist on everyone acknowledging his British blood—and like any Greek man, indeed any *man* he had an inborn need to be the one in control.

His claim to be in love with this other woman was simply his way of showing that control, rejecting the marriage to her which was so very dear to his grandfather's heart and to her own.

As the limousine sped away from the kerb she leaned forward and gave the driver the address of a prestigious apartment block overlooking the river. She herself did not maintain a home in London; she preferred New York's social life and the Paris shops.

Andreas might think he had outmanoeuvred her by announcing his engagement to this undoubtedly cold and sexless English fiancée. Well, she would soon bring an end to that, and make sure that he knew where his real interests lay. After all, how could he possibly resist *her*? She had everything he could want, and he certainly had everything *she* wanted.

It was a pity he had managed to prevent her from outbidding him for this latest acquisition. Ownership of the hotels themselves meant nothing to her *per se*, but it would have been an excellent bait to dangle in front of him since he obviously set a great deal of store by them. Why, she could not understand. But then in many ways there were a considerable number of things about Andreas that she did not understand. It was one of the things that made him so desirable to her. Athena had always coveted that which seemed to be out of reach.

The first time she had realised she wanted Andreas he had been fifteen and she had been on the verge of marrying her husband. She smiled wantonly to herself, licking her lips. At fifteen Andreas, although a boy, had been as tall as a man and as broad, with a superbly fit young body, and so indescribably good-looking that the sight of him had made her melt with lust.

She had done her best to seduce him but he had managed to resist her and then, within a month of deciding that she wanted him, she had been married.

At twenty-two she had not been a young bride by Greek standards, and she had been carefully stalking her husband-to-be for some time. Older than her by a decade, and immensely wealthy, he had played a cat and mouse game with her for well over a year before he had finally capitulated. There had certainly been no way she was going to give up the marriage she had worked so hard for for the passion she felt for Andreas, a mere boy.

But then fate had stepped in. Her husband had died unexpectedly and she had been left a widow. A very rich widow…a very rich and sexually hungry widow. And Andreas was now a man—and what a man!

The only thing that was keeping them apart was Andreas's pride. It had to be. What other reason could he possibly have for resisting her advances?

As the limousine pulled up at the address she had

given the driver Athena examined her reflection in the neat mirrors fitted into the Rolls's interior. That discreet nip and tuck she had had last year had been well worth the prince's ransom she had paid the American plastic surgeon. She could quite easily pass for a woman in her early thirties now.

Her jet-black hair had been cut and styled by one of the world's top hairdressers, her skin glowed from the expensive creams lavished on it, her make-up was immaculate and emphasised the slanting darkness of her eyes, her toe and fingernails gleamed richly with dark red polish.

A smile of satisfaction curved her mouth. No, there was no way Andreas's dreary little fiancée—an office girl, someone he had supposedly fallen in love with during the negotiations to buy out the hotel chain—could compete with her. Athena's eyes hardened. This girl, whoever she was, would soon learn what a mistake she had made in trying to lay claim on the man *Athena* wanted. What a very, very big mistake!

As she left the limousine the perfume she had especially blended for her in Paris moved with her, a heavy, musky cloud of sexuality.

Her teenage daughters loathed it, and were constantly begging her to change it, but she had no intention of doing so. It was her signature, the essence of herself as a woman. Andreas's English fiancée no doubt wore something dull and insipid such as lavender water!

'I'll leave the car here,' Andreas told Saskia as he swung the Mercedes into a multi-storey car park right in the centre of the city. Saskia's eyes widened as she saw the tariff pinned up by the barrier. She would never have dreamed of paying so much to park a car, but the rich, as they said, were different.

Just how different she came to realise during the course of the afternoon, as Andreas guided her into a series of shops the like of which Saskia had never imagined existed. And in each one the very aura of his presence seemed to draw from the sales assistants the kind of reverential reaction that made Saskia tighten her lips. She could see the female admiration and speculation in their eyes as a series of outfits was produced for his inspection. For *his* inspection—not *hers*, Saskia recognised and her sense of helpless frustration and resentment grew with each shop they visited.

'I'm not a doll or a child,' she exploded outside one of them, when she had flatly refused to even try on the cream trouser suit the salesgirl had gushingly declared would be perfect for her.

'No? Well, you're certainly giving a wonderful imitation of behaving like one,' Andreas responded grimly. 'That suit was—'

'That suit was over one thousand pounds,' Saskia interrupted him grittily. 'There's no *way* I would ever pay that kind of money for an outfit... not even my wedding dress!'

When Andreas started to laugh she glared furiously at him, demanding, 'What's so funny?'

'You are,' he told her uncompromisingly. 'My dear Saskia, have you really any idea of the kind of wedding dress you would get for under a thousand pounds?'

'No, I haven't,' Saskia admitted. 'But I do know that I'd never feel comfortable wearing clothes the cost of which would feed a small country, and neither is an expensive wedding dress any guarantee of a good marriage.'

'Oh, spare me the right-on lectures,' Andreas broke in in exasperation. 'Have you ever thought of how many people would be without jobs if everyone went around wearing sackcloth and ashes, as you obviously would have them do?'

'That's not fair,' Saskia defended herself. She was, after all, feminine enough to like good clothes and to want to look her best, and in that trouser suit she *would* undeniably have looked good, she admitted inwardly. But she was acutely conscious of the fact that every penny Andreas spent on her she would have to repay.

'I don't know why you're insisting on doing this,' she told Andreas rebelliously. 'I don't *need* any clothes; I've already told you that. And there's certainly no need for you to throw your money around to impress me.'

'You or anyone else,' Andreas cut in sharply, dark bands of colour burning across his cheekbones in a visual warning to her that she had angered him.

'I am a businessman, Saskia. Throwing money around for *any* reason is not something I do, least of all in an attempt to impress a woman who could easily be bought for less than half the price of that trouser suit. Oh, no, you don't,' he cautioned her softly, reaching out to catch hold of the hand she had automatically lifted.

He was holding her wrist in such a tight grip that

Saskia could actually see her fingers going white, but her pride wouldn't allow her to tell him that he was hurting her. It also wouldn't allow her to acknowledge that she had momentarily let her feelings get out of control, and it was only when she suddenly started to sway, white-faced with pain and shock, that Andreas realised what was happening. He released her wrist with a muffled curse and then start to chafe life back into her hand.

'Why didn't you *tell* me I was hurting you so much?' he grated. 'You have bones as fragile as a bird's.'

Even now, with his dark head bent over her tingling hand whilst he massaged it expertly to bring the blood stinging back into her veins, Saskia couldn't allow herself to weaken and claim his compassion.

'I didn't want to spoil your fun,' she told him sharply. 'You were obviously *enjoying* hurting me.'

She tensed when she heard the oath he gave as he released her completely, and tensed again at the sternness in his voice, one look of grim determination in his eyes as he said, 'This has gone far enough. You are behaving like a child. First a harlot and now a child. There is only *one* role I want to see you play from now on, Saskia, and that is the one we have already agreed upon. I'll warn you now. If you do or say *anything* to make my family suspect that ours is not a true love match I shall make you very sorry for it. Do you understand me?'

'Yes, I understand you,' Saskia agreed woodenly.

'I mean what I say,' Andreas warned her. 'And it won't just be the Demetrios chain you won't be able to work for. If you flout me, Saskia, I'll see to it that you will never be able to work *anywhere* again. An accountant who can't be trusted and who has been dismissed on suspicion of stealing is not one that anyone will want to employ.'

'You can't do that,' Saskia whispered, white-faced, but she knew all too well that he could.

She hated him now...really hated him, and when in the next shop he marched her into she saw the salesgirl's eyes widening in breathless sexual interest, she reflected mentally that the other girl was welcome to him...more than welcome!

It was late in the afternoon before Andreas finally decided that Saskia had a wardrobe suitable for his fiancée.

At their last port of call he had called upon the services of the store's personal shopper who, with relentless efficiency, had provided Saskia with the kind of clothes that she had previously only ever seen in glossy magazines.

She had tried to reject everything the shopper had produced, but on each occasion apart from one Andreas had overruled her. The only time they had been in accord had been when the shopper had brought out a bikini which she had announced was perfect for Saskia's colouring and destination. The minuteness of the triangles which were supposed to cover her modesty had made Saskia's eyes widen in disbelief—and they had widened even more when she had discreetly managed to study the price tag.

'I couldn't possibly swim in that,' she had blurted out.

'*Swim* in it?' The other woman had looked stunned. 'Good heavens, no, of course not. This isn't for *swimming* in. And, look, this is the wrap that goes with it. Isn't it divine?' she had purred, producing a length of silky fragile fabric embellished with sequins.

As she'd seen the four-figure price on the wrap Saskia had thought she might actually faint with disbelief, but to her relief and surprise Andreas had also shaken his head.

'That is *not* the kind of outfit I would wish my fiancée to wear,' he had told the shopper bluntly, adding, just in case she had not fully understood him, 'Saskia's body is eye-catching enough without her needing to embellish it with an outfit more suitable for a call girl.'

The shopper diplomatically had not pressed the issue, but instead had gone away, returning with several swimsuits.

Saskia had picked the cheapest of them, unwillingly allowing Andreas to add a matching wrap.

Whilst he'd been settling the bill and making arrangements for everything to be delivered to his riverside apartment Saskia had drunk the coffee the personal shopper had organised for her.

Perhaps it was because she hadn't really eaten anything all day that she was feeling so lightheaded and anxious, she decided. It couldn't surely be because she and Andreas were now going to go to his apartment, where they would be alone—could it?

'There's an excellent restaurant close to the apartment block,' Andreas informed Saskia, once they were in the car and he was driving her towards the dockland area where his apartment was situated. 'I'll arrange to have a meal sent in and...'

'No,' Saskia protested immediately. 'I'd rather eat out.'

She could see that Andreas was frowning.

'I don't think that's a good idea,' he told her flatly. 'A woman on her own, especially a woman like you, is bound to attract attention, and besides, you look tired. I have to go out, and I have no idea what time I will be back.'

Andreas was going out. Saskia could feel her anxiety easing. Her feet ached from the unaccustomed pavement-pounding and her brain was exhausted with the effort of keeping a running tab on just how much money Andreas, and therefore she, had spent.

Far more than she had wanted to spend. So much that just thinking about it was making her feel distinctly ill. Wretchedly she acknowledged that there would be precious little left of her hard-earned little nest egg once she had repaid Andreas what he had spent.

Tiredly Saskia followed Andreas through the underground car park and into the foyer of the apartment block. A special key was needed to use the lift, which glided upwards so smoothly that Saskia's eyes rounded in shock when it came to a standstill. She had not even realised that they were moving.

'It's this way,' Andreas told her, touching her arm and guiding her towards one of the four doorways opening off the entrance lobby. He was carrying her case, which he put down as he unlocked the door, motioning to Saskia to precede him into the elegant space beyond it.

CHAPTER FIVE

THE first thing that struck Saskia about Andreas's apartment was not the very expensive modern art hanging on the hallway's walls but its smell—a musky, throat-closing, shockingly overpowering scent which stung her nostrils and made her tense.

That Andreas was equally aware of it she was in no doubt. Saskia could see him pause and lift his head, like a hunting panther sniffing the air.

'Hell... Hell and damnation,' she heard him mutter ferociously beneath his breath, and then, to her shock, he thrust open the door into the huge-windowed living space that lay beyond the lobby and took hold of her. His fingers bit into the soft flesh of her arms, his breath a warning whisper against her lips as his eyes blazed down into the unguarded shocked softness of hers, dark as obsidian, hard as flint, commanding...warning...

'Alone at last. How you have enjoyed teasing me today, my loved one, but now I have you to myself and I can exact what punishment on you I wish...'

The soft crooning tone of his voice as much as his words scattered what was left of her senses, leaving Saskia clinging weakly to him as the shock ripped through her in a floodtide. Then his mouth was covering hers, silencing the protest she was trying to make, his lips moulding, shaping, coaxing, *seducing* hers with an expertise that flattened her defences as effectively as an atom bomb.

Incoherently Saskia whispered his name, trying to insist on a cessation of what he was doing and an explanation for it. But her lips, her mouth, her senses, unused to so much sensual stimulation, were defying reason and caution and everything else that Saskia's bemused brain was trying to tell them. Her frozen shock melted beneath the heat of the pleasure Andreas's hungry passionate expertise was showing her, and her lips softened and trembled into an unguarded, uninhibited response.

Without being aware of what she was doing Saskia strained to get closer to Andreas, standing on tiptoe so that she could cling ardently to the delicious pleasure of his kiss. Her hands on his arms registered the sheer size and inflexibility of the muscles beneath them whilst her heart pounded in awed inexperienced shock at the intensity of what she was feeling.

Even more than she could smell that musky, overpowering female perfume, she could smell Andreas himself. His heat...his passion...his maleness... And shockingly something in her, something she hadn't known existed, was responding to it just as her lips were responding to him...just as *she* was responding to him, swaying into his arms compliantly, her body urging him to draw her close, to let her feel the rest of his male strength.

Dizzily Saskia opened the eyes she had closed at the first touch of his mouth on hers, shivering as she saw the sparks of raw sensuality darting like lightning from his eyes as he stared down at her. It was like hanging way above the earth in a dizzying, death-defying place where she could feel her danger and yet at the same time know somehow she would be safe.

'You love like an innocent…a virgin…' Andreas was telling her huskily, and as he did so the sparks glittering in his eyes intensified, as though he found something very satisfying about such a notion.

Helplessly Saskia stared back at him. Her heart was thudding frantically fast and her body was filled with an unfamiliar shocking ache that was a physical need to have him touch her, to have his hand run slowly over her skin and reach right through it to that place where her unfamiliar ache began, so that he could surround and soothe it. Somehow just thinking about him doing such a thing *increased* the ache to a pounding throb, a wild, primitive beat that made her moan and sway even closer to him.

'You like that… You want me…'

As he spoke to her she could hear and feel the urgency in his voice, could feel his arousal. Eagerly she pressed closer to him, only to freeze as she suddenly heard a woman's voice demanding sharply, 'Andreas? Aren't you going to introduce me?'

Immediately she realised what she was doing and shame flooded through her, but as she tried to pull away, desperate to conceal her confusion, Andreas held on to her, forcing her to stay where she was, forcing her even more closely into his body so that somehow she was leaning against him, as though…as though…

She trembled as she felt the powerful thrust of his leg between her own, her face burning hotly with embarrassed colour as she realised the sexual connotation that their pose suggested. But it seemed that the woman who was watching them was not similarly self-conscious.

Saskia caught her breath as Andreas allowed her to turn her head and look at the woman.

She was tall and dark-haired, everything about her immaculately groomed, but despite the warmth of her olive skin and the ripe richness of her painted mouth and nails Saskia shivered as she sensed her innate coldness.

'Athena,' Andreas was demanding shortly, 'how did *you* get in here?'

'I have a key. Have you forgotten?' the other woman purred.

The sloe-eyed look she gave Andreas and the way she was managing to totally exclude Saskia both from their conversation and from her line of vision left Saskia ruefully reflecting on her earlier mental picture of a devastated widow being too grief-stricken at the loss of her husband to prevent herself from being bullied into a second marriage.

No one would ever bully *this* woman into any-thing…and as for her being grief-stricken—there was only one emotion Saskia could see in those dark eyes and it had nothing to do with grief.

She forced down the sudden surge of nausea that burned in her throat as she witnessed the look of pure condensed lust that Athena was giving Andreas. Saskia had never imagined, never mind seen, a woman looking at a man in such a powerfully and openly predatory sexual way.

Now she could understand why Andreas had felt in need of a mock fiancée to protect himself, but what she could not understand was how on earth Andreas could resist the other woman's desire for him.

She was blindingly sensually attractive, and obviously wanted Andreas. And surely that was what all men fantasised about—a woman whose sexual appetite for them could never be satiated.

Naively Saskia assumed that only her own sex would be put off by Athena's intrinsic coldness and by the lack of any real loving emotion in her make-up.

Andreas had obviously kissed Saskia because he had guessed that Athena was in the apartment, and now that the other woman was standing so close to them both Saskia knew how he had known. That perfume of hers was as unmistakable as it was unappealing.

'Aren't you going to say how pleased you are to see me?' Athena was pouting as she moved closer to Andreas. 'Your grandfather is very upset about your engagement. You know what he was hoping for,' she added meaningfully, before turning to Saskia and saying dismissively, 'Oh, I'm sorry. I didn't mean to hurt your feelings, but I'm sure Andreas must have warned you how difficult it is going to be for all his family, especially for his grandfather, to accept you...'

'Athena,' Andreas was saying warningly, and Saskia could well imagine how she *would* have felt to be confronted by such a statement, if she and Andreas were genuinely engaged.

'But it's the truth,' Athena was continuing unrepentantly, and she shrugged her shoulders, the movement drawing attention to the fullness of her breasts. Breasts which Saskia could quite easily see were naked and unfettered beneath the fine cotton shirt she was wearing.

Quickly she averted her gaze from the sight of Athena's flauntingly erect nipples, not daring to allow herself to look at Andreas. Surely no man could resist the demand that those nipples were making on his attention...his concentration...his admiration for their perfection and sexuality. Her own breasts were well shaped and firm, but her nipples did not have that flamboyant fullness that the other woman's possessed and, even if they had, Saskia knew that she would have felt embarrassed about making such a public display of them.

But then perhaps Athena's display was meant *only* for Andreas...perhaps it was meant to be a reminder to him of intimacies they might already have shared. She did, after all, have the key to his apartment, and she certainly seemed to want to make it plain to Saskia that there was a very special intimacy between the two of them.

As though in confirmation of Saskia's thoughts, Athena suddenly leaned forward, putting one manicured hand against Andreas's face and effectively coming between them. With a sultry suggestiveness she said softly, 'Aren't you going to kiss me? You normally do, and I'm sure your fiancée understands that in Greece family relationships...family *loyalties* are very, very important.'

'What Saskia understands is that I love her and I want her to be my wife,' Andreas informed Athena curtly, stepping back from her and taking Saskia with him. As he held her in front of him and closed his arms around her, tucking her head against his shoulder, Saskia reminded herself just *why* he was doing so and just what her role was supposed to be.

'How sweet!' Athena pronounced, giving Saskia an icy look before turning back to Andreas and telling him insincerely, 'I hate to cast a shadow on your happiness, Andreas, but your grandfather really isn't very pleased with you at all at the moment. He was telling me how concerned he is about the way you're handling this recent takeover. Of course *I* understand how important it must be to you to establish your own mark on the business, to prove yourself, so to speak, but the acquisition of this hotel chain really was quite foolhardy, as is this decision of yours to keep on all the existing staff.

'You'll never make a profit doing that,' she scolded him mock sweetly. 'I must say, though, having had the opportunity to look a little deeper into the finances of the chain, I'm glad I pulled out of putting in my own bid. Although of course I *can* afford to lose the odd million or so. What a pity it is, Andreas, that you didn't accept my offer to run the shipping line for me. That would have given you much more scope than working as your grandfather's errand boy.'

Saskia felt herself tensing as she absorbed the insult Athena had just delivered, but to her astonishment Andreas seemed completely unmoved by it. Yet *she* only had to make the merest observation and he fired up at her with so much anger.

'As you already well know, Athena,' he responded, almost good-humouredly, 'It was my *grandfather's* decision to buy the British hotel chain and it was one I endorsed. As for its future profitability... My research confirms that there is an excellent market for a chain of luxurious hotels in Britain, especially when it can boast first-class leisure facilities and a top-notch chef—which is what I am going to ensure that our chain has.

'And as for the financial implications of keeping on the existing staff—Saskia is an accountant, and I'm sure she'll be able to tell you—as you should know yourself, being a businesswoman—that in the long run it would cost more in redundancy payments to get rid of the staff than it will cost to continue employing them. Natural wastage and pending retirement will reduce their number quite dramatically over the next few years, and, where appropriate, those who wish to stay on will be given the opportunity to relocate and retrain. The leisure clubs we intend to open in each hotel alone will take up virtually all of the slack in our staffing levels.

'However, Saskia and I are leaving for Athens tomorrow. We've had a busy day today and, if you'll excuse us, tonight is going to be a very special night for us.'

As Saskia tensed Andreas tightened his hold on her warningly as he repeated, 'A *very* special night. Which reminds me...'

Still holding onto Saskia with one hand, he reached inside his jacket pocket with the other to remove a small jeweller's box.

'I collected this. It should be small enough for you now.'

Before Saskia could say anything he was slipping

the box back into his jacket, telling her softly, 'We'll find out later…'

In the living area beyond the lobby a telephone had started to ring. Releasing her, Andreas went to answer it, leaving Saskia on her own with Athena.

'It won't last,' Athena told her venomously as she walked past Saskia towards the door. 'He won't marry you. He and I were destined to be together. He *knows* that. It's just his pride that makes him fight his destiny. You might as well give him up now, because I promise you *I* shall never do so.'

She meant it, Saskia could see that, and for the first time she actually felt a small shaft of sympathy for Andreas. Sympathy for a man who was treating her the way Andreas was? For a man who had misjudged her the way he had? She must be crazy, Saskia derided herself grimly.

Apprehensively Saskia watched as the new suitcases, which were now carefully packed with her new clothes, were loaded onto the conveyor belt. The airline representative was checking their passports.

On her finger the ring Andreas had given her the previous evening glittered brilliantly.

'It's amazing how good fake diamonds can look these days, isn't it?' she had chattered nervously when Andreas had taken it from its box. She'd tried to disguise from him how edgy and unhappy she felt about wearing a ring on the finger that she had imagined would only ever bear a ring given to her by the man she loved, a ring she would wear forever.

'Is it?' Andreas had responded almost contemptuously. 'I wouldn't know.'

His comment had set all her inner alarm bells ringing and she had demanded anxiously, 'This... It isn't real, is it?'

His expression had given her her answer.

'It *is*!' She had swallowed, unable to drag her gaze away from the fiery sparkle of the magnificent solitaire.

'Athena would have spotted a fake diamond immediately,' Andreas had told her dismissively when she'd tried to protest that she didn't want the responsibility of wearing something of such obvious value.

'If she can spot a fake *diamond* so easily,' she had felt driven to ask him warily, 'then surely she will be able to spot a fake fiancée.'

'Athena deals in hard facts, not emotions,' had been Andreas's answer.

Hard facts, Saskia reflected now, remembering that brief conversation. Like the kiss Andreas had given her last night, knowing Athena would witness it. Andreas himself had made no mention of what he had done, but Saskia had known that her guess as to why he had done it was correct when, immediately after he had ended his telephone call, he had switched on the apartment's air conditioning with the grim comment, 'We need some fresh air in here.'

Later, Andreas had gone out, as promised, and, after picking at the meal he had ordered her, Saskia had gone to bed—alone.

'How long will it take us to reach Aphrodite?' Saskia asked Andreas as they boarded their flight.

'On this occasion it will take longer than normal,'

Andreas answered as the stewardess showed them to their seats—first-class seats, Saskia noted with a small frisson of nervous awe. She had never flown first class before, never really done anything that might have equipped her to feel at home in the rarefied stratosphere of the mega-wealthy that Andreas and his family obviously inhabited.

'Once we arrive in Athens I'm afraid I shall have to leave you to occupy yourself for a few hours before we continue with our journey. That was my grandfather who rang last night. He wants to see me.'

'He won't be at the island?' Saskia asked.

'Not immediately. His heart condition means that he has to undergo regular check-ups—a precautionary measure only, thank goodness—and they will keep him in Athens for the next day or so.'

'Athena told me she doesn't believe that our relationship will last. She believes that the two of you are destined to be together,' Saskia said.

'She's trying to intimidate you,' Andreas responded, the smile he had given the attentive stewardess replaced by a harsh frown.

Impulsively Saskia allowed the sympathy she had unexpectedly felt for him the previous evening to take precedence over her own feelings. Turning towards him, she said softly, 'But surely if you explained to your grandfather how you feel he would understand and accept that you can't be expected to marry a woman you don't...you don't want to marry...'

'My grandfather is as stubborn as a mule. He's also one hell of a lot more vulnerable than he thinks...than any of us want him to think. His heart condition...' He gave a small sigh. 'At the moment it's stable, but it is important that he—and we—keep his stress levels down. If I told him that I didn't want to marry Athena without producing you as a substitute he would immediately become very stressed indeed. It isn't just that by marrying Athena as he wishes I would attach her fortune and assets to our own, my grandfather is also a man to whom male descendants are of paramount importance.

'My elder sister already has two daughters, and Athena also has two. My grandfather is desperate for me, as his direct male descendent, to produce the next male generation...a great-grandson.'

'But even if you did marry Athena there would be no guarantee that you would even have children, never mind sons,' Saskia protested.

'Why are you laughing at me?' she demanded in chagrin as she saw the mirth crinkling Andreas's eyes and a gust of warmly amused male laughter filled the small space between them.

'Saskia, for a woman of your experience you can be very, very naïve. You should *never* suggest to any man, and most *especially* not a Greek one, that he may not be able to father a son!'

As the plane suddenly started to lift into the sky Saskia automatically clutched at her arm-rests, and then tensed in shock as she felt the hard male warmth of Andreas's hand wrapping around her own.

'Scared of flying?' he asked her in amusement. 'You shouldn't be. It's the safest form of transport there is.'

'I know that,' Saskia responded waspishly. 'It's

just…well, it's just that flying seems so…so unnatural, and if…'

'If God had intended man to fly he'd have given him wings,' Andreas offered her wryly. 'Well, Icarus tried that option.'

'I always think that's such a sad story.' Saskia shivered, her eyes shadowing. 'Especially for his poor father.'

'Mmm…' Andreas agreed, before asking her, 'Am I to take it from that comment that you're a student of Greek mythology?'

'Well, not precisely a student,' Saskia admitted, 'but my grandmother used to read me stories from a book on Greek mythology when I was little and I always found the stories fascinating…even though they nearly always made me cry.'

Abruptly she stopped speaking as she realised two things. The first was that they were now completely airborne, and the second was…her own bemused awareness of how good it felt actually to have Andreas's large hand clasping her own. It was enough to make her face sting with self-conscious colour and she hastily wriggled her hand free, just as the stewardess came up to offer them a glass of champagne.

'Champagne!' Saskia's eyes widened as she took a sip from the glass Andreas was holding out to her and she gasped as the delicious bubbles exploded against her taste buds.

It had to be the champagne that was making her feel so relaxed and so…so…laid-back, Saskia decided hazily a little later, and when the captain announced that they were coming in to land she was

surprised to realise how quickly the time had flown—
and how much she had enjoyed the conversation she
and Andreas had shared. She was even more surprised to discover how easy it was to slip her hand
into the reassuring hold of Andreas's as the plane's
wheels hit the tarmac and the pilot applied reverse
thrust to slow them down.

'I can either have our driver take you to the family
apartment in Athens, where you can rest whilst I see
my grandfather, or, if you prefer, I can arrange for
him to drive you on a sightseeing tour,' Andreas offered, casually lifting their cases off the luggage car-
ousel.

He was wearing a pair of plain light-coloured trousers and a cool, very fine white cotton short-sleeved
shirt, and for some indefinable reason it did odd
things to Saskia's normally very sensible female
senses to witness the way the muscles hardened in
his arms as he swung their cases on to the ground.
Very odd things, she acknowledged giddily as the
discreet smile of flirtatious invitation she intercepted
from a solitary woman traveller caused her instinctively to move possessively closer to him.

What on earth was happening to her? It *must* be
the champagne…or the heat…or perhaps both! Yes,
that was it, she decided feverishly, grateful to have
found a sensible explanation for her unfamiliar behaviour. After all, there was no reason why she
should feel possessive about Andreas. Yesterday
morning she had hated him…loathed him… In fact
she had been dreading her enforced time as his 'fiancée'—and she still was, of course. Of course! It
was just that…

Well, having met Athena it was only natural that she should feel *some* sympathy for him. And she had been fascinated by the stories he had told her during the flight—stories which had been told to him by older members of his Greek family and which were a wonderful mix of myth and folklore. And it was a very pleasant experience not to have to struggle with heavy luggage. Normally when she went away she was either with a group of friends or with her grand-mother, and...

'Saskia...?'

Guiltily Saskia realised that Andreas was still waiting for an answer to his question.

'Oh, I'd much prefer to see something of the city,' she answered.

'Well, you won't have a lot of time,' Andreas warned her. 'Our pilot will already have filed his flight plan.'

Saskia already knew that they would be flying out to the island in a small plane privately owned by Andreas's grandfather, and what had impressed her far more than Andreas's casual reference to the plane had been his mention of the fact that he himself was qualified to fly.

'Unfortunately I had to give it up. I can't spare the amount of hours now that I believe are needed to keep myself up to speed and in practice, and be-sides, my insurance company were extremely wary about insuring me,' he'd added ruefully.

'It's this way,' he told her now, placing his hand on her shoulder as he turned her in the right direc-tion.

Out of the corner of her eye Saskia caught a

glimpse of their reflections in a mirrored column and immediately tensed. What was she *doing* leaning against Andreas like that? As though…as though she *liked* being there…as though she was enjoying playing the helpless fragile female to his strong muscular male.

Immediately she pulled away from him and squared her shoulders.

'Athena would have loved to have seen you do that,' he told her sharply, the disapproval clear in his voice.

'We're supposed to be in love, Saskia…remember?'

'Athena isn't here,' she responded quickly.

'No, thank God,' he agreed. 'But we don't know who might accidentally observe us. We're a *couple*— very much in love—newly engaged…and you're about to fly to my home to meet my family. Don't you think it's natural that—?'

'That I should feel nervous and intimidated…worried about whether or not they'll think I'm good enough for you.' Saskia interrupted him angrily, her pride stung by what he was suggesting. 'And what am I supposed to do? Cling desperately and despairingly to you…afraid of their rejection…afraid of *losing* you…just because—'

She stopped as she saw the blank impatient look Andreas was giving her.

'What I was about to say,' he told her grimly, 'was don't you think it's only natural that I should want to hold you close to me and equally that *you* should want that same intimacy? That as lovers we *should* want always to be physically in touch with one another?' He paused. 'And as for what you have just said, I'm a man of thirty-five, long past the age of needing *anyone's* approval of what I do or who I love.'

'But you don't…' Saskia began, and then stopped as she realised what she had been about to say. Andreas hardly needed *her* to tell him that he didn't love her.

'I don't what?' he prompted her, but she shook her head, refusing to answer him.

'So you want to see the Acropolis first?' Andreas checked with Saskia before getting out of the limousine, having first given the driver some instructions in Greek.

'Yes,' Saskia confirmed.

'I have told Spiros to make sure you are at the airport in time for our flight. He will take care of you. I am sorry to have to leave you to your own devices,' Andreas apologised formally, suddenly making Saskia sharply aware of his mixed cultural heritage.

She recognised how at home he looked here, and yet, at the same time, how much he stood out from the other men she could see. He was taller, for one thing, and his skin, whilst tanned, was not as dark, and of course his eyes would always give away his Northern European blood.

Saskia gave a small emotional sigh as she finally turned her back on the Acropolis and started to walk away. She had managed to persuade the driver that she would be perfectly safe on her own, but only after a good deal of insistence, and she had enjoyed her solitude as she had absorbed the aura of the ancient building in awed appreciation.

Now, though, it was time for her to go. She could see the limousine waiting where she had expected, but to her consternation there was no sign of its driver.

There *was* a man standing close to the vehicle, though, white-haired and elderly. Saskia frowned as she recognised that he seemed to be in some distress, one hand pressed against his side as though he was in pain. A brief examination of the street confirmed that it was empty, apart from the old man and herself. Saskia automatically hurried towards him, anxious for his well-being.

'Are you all right?' she asked in concern as she reached him. 'You don't look well.'

To her relief he answered her in English, assuring her, 'It is nothing...the heat—a small pain. I have perhaps walked further than I should...'

Saskia was still anxious. It *was* hot. He did not look well, and there was certainly no way she could possibly leave him on his own, but there was still no sign of her driver or anyone else who might be able to help, and she had no idea how long it would take them to get to the airport.

'It's *very* hot,' she told the old man gently, not wanting to hurt his pride, 'and it can be very tiring to walk in such heat. I have a car...and...and a driver... Perhaps we could give you a lift?' As she spoke she was searching the street anxiously. Where *was* her driver? Andreas would be furious with her if she was late for their flight, but there was no way she could leave without first ensuring that the old man was alright.

'You have a car? This car?' he guessed, gesturing towards the parked limousine.

'Well, it isn't *mine*,' Saskia found herself feeling obliged to tell him. 'It belongs to...to someone I know. Do you live very far away?'

He had stopped holding his side now and she could see that his colour looked healthier and that his breathing was easier.

'You are very kind,' he told her with a smile, 'But I too have a car...and a driver...' His smile broadened and for some reason Saskia felt almost as though he was laughing a little at her.

'You are a very kind girl to worry yourself so much on behalf of an old man.'

There *was* a car parked further down the street, Saskia realised, but it was some distance away.

'Is *that* your car?' she asked him. 'Shall I get the driver?'

'No,' he denied immediately. 'I can walk.'

Without giving him any opportunity to refuse, Saskia went to his side and said gently, 'Perhaps you will allow me to walk with you to it...' Levelly she met and held the look he was giving her.

'Perhaps I should,' he capitulated.

It took longer to reach the car than Saskia had expected, mainly because the old man was plainly in more distress than he wanted to admit. As they reached the car Saskia was relieved to see the driver's door open and the driver get out, immediately hurrying towards them and addressing some words to her companion in fast Greek. The old man was now starting to look very much better, holding himself upright and speaking sternly to the driver.

'He fusses like an old woman,' he complained testily in English to Saskia, adding warmly, 'Thank you, my dear, I am *very* pleased to have met you. But you should not be walking the streets of Athens on your own,' he told her sternly. 'And I shall—' Abruptly he stopped and said something in Greek to his driver, who started to frown and look anxiously up and down the street.

'Yannis will walk back with you to *your* car and wait there with you until your driver returns.'

'Really, there's no need for that,' Saskia protested, but her new-found friend was determinedly insistent.

'There really is no need for you to come with me,' she told the driver once they were out of earshot of the older man. 'I would much rather you stayed with your employer. He looked quite poorly when I saw him in the street.'

To her relief, as she finished speaking she saw that her own driver was getting out of Andreas's car.

'See, there is no need to come any further,' she smiled in relief, and then frowned a little before saying anxiously to him, 'Your employer... It is none of my business I know...but perhaps a visit to a doctor...' She paused uncertainly.

'It is already taken care of,' the driver assured her. 'But he... What do you say? He does not always take anyone's advice...'

His calmness helped to soothe Saskia's concern and ease her conscience about leaving the older man. He was plainly in good hands now, and her own driver was waiting for her.

CHAPTER SIX

SASKIA darted a brief look at Andreas, catching back her gasp of pleasure as she stared out of their plane and down at the blue-green of the Aegean Sea beneath them.

He had been frowning and preoccupied when they had met up at the airport, not even asking her if she had enjoyed her sightseeing trip, and now with every mile that took them closer to his home and family Saskia could feel her tension increasing. It seemed ironic, when she reflected on how she had dreamed of one day spending a holiday in this part of the world, that now that she was actually here she was far too on edge to truly appreciate it.

The starkness of Andreas's expression forced her to ask, more out of politeness than any real concern, she was quick to assure herself, 'Is something wrong? You don't look very happy.'

Immediately Andreas's frown deepened, his gaze sweeping her sharply as he turned to look at her.

'Getting in some practice at playing the devoted fiancée?' he asked her cynically. 'If you're looking for a bonus payment, don't bother.'

Saskia felt a resurgence of her initial hostility towards him.

'Unlike you, I do not evaluate everything I do by how I can best benefit from it,' Saskia shot back

Play The Lucky Hearts Game

and get...
FREE BOOKS & a FREE GIFT...
YOURS to KEEP!

Yes! I have scratched off the silver card. Please send me my **2 FREE BOOKS** and **FREE MYSTERY GIFT**. I understand that I am under no obligation to purchase any books as explained on the back of this card.

Scratch Here!
then look below to see
what your cards get you...

306 HDL DC3W   **106 HDL DC3M**

NAME   (PLEASE PRINT CLEARLY)

ADDRESS

APT.#   CITY

STATE/PROV.   ZIP/POSTAL CODE

Twenty-one gets you
2 FREE BOOKS and a
FREE MYSTERY GIFT!

Twenty gets you
2 FREE BOOKS!

Nineteen gets you
1 FREE BOOK!

TRY AGAIN!

DETACH AND MAIL CARD TODAY!

Visit us online at
www.eHarlequin.com

The Harlequin Reader Service® — Here's how it works:

Accepting your 2 free books and gift places you under no obligation to buy anything. You may keep the books and gift and return the shipping statement marked "cancel." If you do not cancel, about a month later we'll send you 6 additional novels and bill you just $3.34 each in the U.S., or $3.74 each in Canada, plus 25¢ shipping & handling per book and applicable taxes if any.* That's the complete price and — compared to cover prices of $3.99 each in the U.S. and $4.50 each in Canada — it's quite a bargain! You may cancel at any time, but if you choose to continue, every month we'll send you 6 more books, which you may either purchase at the discount price or return to us and cancel your subscription.

*Terms and prices subject to change without notice. Sales tax applicable in N.Y. Canadian residents will be charged applicable provincial taxes and GST.

If offer card is missing write to: Harlequin Reader Service, 3010 Walden Ave., P.O. Box 1867, Buffalo NY 14240-1867

BUSINESS REPLY MAIL
FIRST-CLASS MAIL   PERMIT NO. 717   BUFFALO, NY

POSTAGE WILL BE PAID BY ADDRESSEE

HARLEQUIN READER SERVICE
3010 WALDEN AVE
PO BOX 1867
BUFFALO NY 14240-9952

NO POSTAGE
NECESSARY
IF MAILED
IN THE
UNITED STATES

furiously. 'I was simply concerned that your meeting hadn't gone very well.'

'*You*? Concerned for *me*? There's only one reason you're here with me, Saskia, and we both know that isn't it.'

What did he expect? Saskia fumed, forcing herself to bite back the angry retort she wanted to make. He had, after all, blackmailed her into being here with him. He was using her for his own ends. He had formed the lowest kind of opinion of her, judged her without allowing her the chance to defend herself or to explain her behaviour, and yet after all that he still seemed to think he could occupy the higher moral ground. Why on earth had she ever felt any sympathy for him? He and Athena deserved one another.

But even as she formed the stubborn angry thought Saskia knew that it wasn't true. She had sensed a deep coldness in Athena, a total lack of regard for any kind of emotion. Andreas might have done and said many things she objected to, but there was a warmly passionate side to him...a *very* passionate side, she acknowledged, trembling a little as she unwillingly remembered the kiss he had given her... Even though it had merely been an act, staged for Athena's benefit he had still made her feel—*connected* at a very deep and personal level. So much so, in fact, that even now, if she were to close her eyes and remember, she could almost feel the hard male pressure of his mouth against her own.

'As a matter of fact my meeting did *not* go well.'

Saskia's eyes opened in surprise as she heard Andreas's abrupt and unexpected admission.

'For a start my grandfather was not there. There

was something else he had to do that was more important, apparently. But unfortunately he did not bother to explain this to me, or to send a message informing me of it until I'd been waiting for him for over half an hour. However, he *had* left instructions that I was to be informed in no uncertain terms that he is not best pleased with me at the moment.'

'Because of me...us?' Saskia hazarded.

'My grandfather knows there is no way I would or could marry a woman I do not love—his own marriage was a love match, as was my parents', even if my mother did have to virtually threaten to elope before she got his approval. When my father died my grandfather admitted how much he admired him. He was a surveyor, and he retained his independence from my grandfather.'

'You must miss him,' Saskia said softly.

'I was fifteen when he died; that was a long time ago. And, unlike you, at least I had the comfort of knowing how much he loved me.'

At first Saskia thought he was being deliberately unkind to her, and instinctively she stiffened in self-defence, but when unexpectedly he covered her folded hands with one of his own she knew that she had misinterpreted his remark.

'The love my grandmother has given me has more than made up for the love I didn't get from my parents,' she told him firmly—and meant it.

His hand was still covering hers...both of hers...and that funny, trembly sensation she had felt inside earlier returned as she looked down at it. Long-fingered, tanned, with well-groomed but not manicured nails, it was very much a man's hand:

large enough to cover both of hers, large enough, too, to hold her securely to him without any visible effort. It was the kind of hand that gave a woman the confidence to know that this man could take care of her and their children. Just as he was the kind of man who would always ensure that his woman and his child were safe and secure.

What on earth was she thinking? Agitatedly Saskia wriggled in her seat, snatching her hands from beneath Andreas's.

'Are you sure this is a good idea?' she asked him slightly breathlessly as she tried to concentrate on the reality of why she was sitting here next to him. 'I mean, if your grandfather already doesn't approve of our engagement...'

It was so long before he replied that Saskia began to think that her question had annoyed him but when he did answer her she recognised that the anger she could see darkening his eyes wasn't directed at her but at Athena.

'Unfortunately Athena claims a blood closeness to my grandfather which he finds flattering. His elder brother, Athena's grandfather, died some years ago and whilst there is no way at all that Athena would allow anyone, least of all my grandfather, to interfere in the way she runs her own financial empire, she flatters and encourages him to the point where his judgement is sometimes not all that it should be. My mother claims that the truth will out, so to speak, and that ultimately my grandfather will see through Athena's machinations.'

'But surely she must realise that you don't want to marry her,' Saskia suggested a little bit uncomfortably. It was so foreign to her own way of behaving to even consider trying to force anyone into a relationship with her that it was hard for her to understand why Athena should be driven to do so.

'Oh, she realises it all right,' Andreas agreed grimly. 'But Athena has never been denied anything she wants, and right now...'

'She wants you,' Saskia concluded for him.

'Yes,' Andreas agreed heavily. 'And, much as I would like to tell her that her desires are not reciprocated, I have to think of my grandfather.'

He stopped speaking as their plane started to lose height, a small smile curling his mouth as he saw Saskia's expression when she looked out of the window down at their destination.

'He can't possibly be intending to put this plane down on that tiny piece of land,' she gasped in disbelief.

'Oh, yes, he can, It's much safer than it looks,' Andreas said reassuringly. 'Look,' he added, directing her attention away from the landing strip and to the breathtaking sprawl of his family villa and the grounds enclosing it.

'Everything is so green,' Saskia told him in bemusement, her eyes widening over the almost perfect oval shape of the small island, the rich green of its gardens and foliage perfectly shown off by the whiteness of its sandy beaches and the wonderful turquoise of the Aegean Sea that lapped them.

'That's because the island has its own plentiful supply of water,' Andreas told her. 'It's far too small to be able to sustain either crops or livestock, which is why it was uninhabited—as you can see it is quite some distance from any of the other islands, the furthest out into the Aegean.'

'It looks perfect,' Saskia breathed. 'Like a pearl drop.'

Andreas laughed, but there was an emotion in his eyes that made Saskia's cheeks flush a little as he told her quietly, 'That was how my grandmother used to describe it.'

Saskia gave a small gasp as the plane suddenly bumped down onto the runway, belatedly realising that Andreas had deliberately distracted her attention away from their imminent landing. He could be so entertaining when he wanted to be, so charming and so easy to be with. A little wistfully she wondered how much difference it would have made to his opinion of her had they met under different circumstances. Then she very firmly pulled her thoughts into order, warning herself that her situation was untenable enough already without making it worse by indulging in ridiculous fantasies and daydreams.

There was a bleak look in Andreas's eyes as he guided Saskia towards the aircraft's exit. There was such a vast contradiction in the way he was perceiving Saskia now and the way he had perceived her the first time he had seen her. For his own emotional peace of mind and security he found himself wishing that she had remained true to his first impression of her. That vulnerability she fought so determinedly and with such pride to conceal touched him in all the ways that a woman of Athena's coldness could never possibly do. Saskia possessed a warmth, a humanity, a womanliness, that his maleness reacted and responded to in the most potentially dangerous way.

Grimly Andreas tried not to allow himself to think about how he had felt when he had kissed her. Initially he had done so purely as an instinctive response to his awareness that Athena was in his apartment—that appalling overpowering scent of hers was instantly recognisable. Quite how she had got hold of a key he had no idea, but he suspected she must have somehow cajoled it from his grandfather. But the kiss he had given Saskia as a means of reinforcing his unavailability to Athena had unexpectedly and unwontedly shown him—*forced* him to acknowledge—something he was still fighting hard to deny.

He didn't *want* to want Saskia. He didn't want it at all, and he certainly didn't want to feel his current desire to protect and reassure her.

Athens had been hot, almost stiflingly so, but here on the island the air had a silky balminess to it that was totally blissful, Saskia decided, shading her eyes from the brilliance of the sun as she reached the ground and looked a little uncertainly at the trio of people waiting to greet them.

Andreas's husky, 'Here you are, darling, you forgot these,' as he handed her a pair of sunglasses threw her into even more confusion, but nowhere near as much as the warm weight of his arm around her as he drew her closer to him and whispered quite audibly, 'Our harsh sunlight is far too strong for those beautiful Celtic eyes of yours.'

Saskia felt her fingers start to tremble as she took the sunglasses from him. They carried a designer logo, she noticed, and were certainly far more expensive than any pair of sunglasses she had ever owned. When Andreas took them back and gently slipped them on for her she discovered that they fitted her perfectly.

'I remembered that we didn't get any in London and I knew you'd need a pair,' he told her quietly, leaning forward to murmur the words into her ear, one arm still around her body and his free hand holding her shoulder as though he would draw her even closer.

To their onlookers they must look very intimate, Saskia recognised, which was no doubt why Andreas had chosen to give them to her in such a manner.

Well, two could play at that game. Without stopping to think about the implications of what she was doing, or to question why she was doing so, Saskia slid her own arm around *his* neck, turning her face up to his as she murmured back, 'Thank you, darling. You really are so thoughtful.'

She had, she recognised on a small spurt of defiant pleasure, surprised him. She could see it in his eyes—and she could see something else as well, something very male and dangerous which made her disengage herself from him hastily and step back. Not that he allowed her to go very far. Somehow he was holding her hand and refusing to let go of it, drawing her towards the small waiting group.

'Mama. This is Saskia...' he announced, introducing Saskia first to the older of the two women.

Warily Saskia studied her, knowing that if she and Andreas were really in love and engaged her heart would be in her mouth as she waited to see whether or not she and Andreas's mother could build a true bond. Physically she looked very much like Athena, although, of course, older. But the similarity ended once Saskia looked into her eyes and saw the warmth there that had been so markedly lacking from Athena's.

There was also a gentleness and sweetness about Andreas's mother, a timidity almost, and intuitively Saskia sensed that she was a woman who, having loved only one man, would never totally cease mourning his loss.

'It's a pleasure to meet you, Mrs Latimer,' Saskia began, but immediately Andreas's mother shook her head chidingly.

'You are going to be my daughter-in-law, Saskia, you must call me something less formal. Helena is my name, or if you wish you may call me Mama, as 'Reas and my daughters do.' As she spoke she leaned forward and placed her hands gently on Saskia's upper arms.

'She is lovely, 'Reas,' she told her son warmly.

'I certainly think so, Mama,' Andreas agreed with a smile.

'I meant inside as well as out,' his mother told him softly.

'And so did I,' Andreas agreed, equally emotionally.

Heavens, but he was a wonderful actor, Saskia acknowledged shakily. If she hadn't known how he really felt about her that look of tender adoration he had given her just now would have…could have… A man like him should know better than to give a vulnerable woman a look like that, she decided indignantly, forgetting for the moment that so far as Andreas was concerned she was anything *but* vulnerable.

'And this is Olympia, my sister,' Andreas continued, turning Saskia towards the younger of the two women. Although she was as darkly Greek as her mother, she too had light coloured eyes and a merry open smile that made Saskia warm instantly to her.

'Heavens, but it's hot down here. Poor Saskia must be melting,' Olympia sympathised.

'You could have waited for us at the villa,' Andreas told her. 'It would have been enough just to have sent a driver with the Land Rover.'

'No, it wouldn't,' Olympia told him starkly, shrugging her shoulders as her mother made a faint sound of protest. She looked anxiously at her, saying, 'Well, he has to know...'

'I have to know what?' Andreas began to frown.

'Athena is here,' his mother told him unhappily. 'She arrived earlier and she...'

'She what?'

'She said that your grandfather had invited her,' his mother continued.

'You know what that means, don't you Andreas?' Olympia interrupted angrily. 'It means that she's bullied Grandfather into saying she could stay. And that's not all...'

'Pia...' her mother began unhappily, but Olympia refused to be silenced.

'She's brought that revolting creep Aristotle with her. She claims that she is right in the middle of an important business deal and that she needs him with her because he's her accountant. If it's so important, how come she had time to be here?' Olympia demanded. 'Oh, but I hate her so. This morning she went on and on about how concerned Grandfather is about the business and how he's been asking her advice because he's worried that you...'

'Pia!' her mother protested again, and this time Andreas's sister did fall silent, but only for a few seconds.

'What I can't understand is why Gramps is so taken in by her,' she burst out, as though unable to contain herself. 'It's obvious what she's doing. She's just trying to get at you, Andreas, because you won't marry her.'

'I'm sorry about this,' Helena Latimer was apologising gently to Saskia. 'It can't be pleasant for you. You haven't met Athena yet, I know—'

'Yes, she has,' Andreas interrupted his mother, explaining when both she and Pia looked at him questioningly, 'Somehow or other she managed to get a key for the London apartment.'

'She's the worst, isn't she?' Pia told Saskia. 'The black widow spider I call her.'

'Pia!' Andreas chided her sharply.

'Mama hasn't told you everything yet,' Pia countered, looking protectively at her mother before continuing, 'Athena has insisted on having the room that Mama had arranged to be prepared for Saskia. It's the one next to your suite—.'

'I tried to stop her, Andreas,' Helena interrupted her daughter unhappily. 'But you know what she's like.'

'She said that Saskia could have the room right down at the end of the corridor. You know, the one we only use as an overspill when absolutely everyone is here. It hasn't even got a proper bed.'

'You'll have to say something to Athena, Andreas.

Make her understand that she can't…that she can't have that room because Saskia will be using it.'

'No, she won't,' Andreas contradicted his mother flatly, sliding his arm very firmly around Saskia, imprisoningly almost, drawing her right into his body so that her face was concealed from view as he told his mother and sister, 'Saskia will be sharing *my* room…and *my* bed…'

Saskia could sense their shock, even though she could not see their faces. *Now* she knew why he was holding her so tightly, preventing anyone else from seeing her expression or hearing the panicky denial she was trying to make but which was muffled against the fine cotton of his shirt.

There was just no way that she was prepared for anything like this. No way that she could ever be prepared for it. But her attempts to tell Andreas were bringing her into even more intimate contact with him as she tried to look up into his face.

His response to her efforts to attract his attention made the situation even worse, because when he bent his head, as though anxious to listen to what she was saying, her lips inadvertently brushed against his jaw.

It must be a combination of heat and shock that was sending that melting liquid sensation of weakness swooshing through her, Saskia decided dizzily. It certainly couldn't be the feel of Andreas's skin against her lips, nor the dangerous gleam she could see in his narrowed eyes as they glittered down into hers. The arm he had around her moved fractionally, so that the hand that had been resting on her waist was now somehow just beneath the curve of her breast, his fingertips splaying against its soft curve and making her…making her…

'Saskia will be sharing your room!' Pia was breathing, verbalising the shock that Saskia herself felt and that she suspected his mother was too embarrassed to voice.

'We *are* engaged…and soon to be married…' Andreas told his sister smoothly, adding in a much rougher, rawer, spine-tinglingly possessive voice, 'Saskia is mine and I intend to make sure that everyone knows it.'

'Especially Aristotle,' Pia guessed. 'I don't know how Athena can endure him,' she continued shuddering. 'He's like a snake, Saskia. All cold and slimy, with horrid little eyes and clammy hands…'

'Athena endures him because of his skill at "creative" accounting,' Andreas informed his sister dryly.

'You mean he's dishonest,' Pia translated pithily.

'You didn't hear that from me,' Andreas warned her as he started to shepherd all three of them towards the waiting Land Rover.

Whilst they had been talking the driver had loaded their luggage, and as he held the door open for his mother, sister and Saskia to get in Saskia heard Andreas asking him about his family, listening interestedly whilst the driver told him with pride about his son who was at university.

'Grandfather was not very pleased at all when Andreas said that he wanted to use the money our father had left him to help pay for the education of our personal household staff,' Pia told Saskia.

'Pia, you aren't being very fair to your grandfather,' her mother objected.

Andreas had done that? Stubbornly Saskia refused to acknowledge that she was impressed by his philanthropy.

Had he really meant what he had said about them sharing a room? He couldn't have done—could he? Personally she didn't care *where* she slept, even if it was a normally unused bedless room, just so long as she occupied it on her own.

'We have both had a long day and I imagine that Saskia is going to want to have a rest before dinner,' Andreas was saying as the Land Rover pulled up in a cool paved courtyard with a central fountain that sent a musical plume of water up into the air to shower back to earth in millions of tiny teardrops.

'I'll make sure everyone knows that you aren't to be disturbed,' his mother responded. 'But perhaps Saskia would like something light to eat and drink…'

Before Saskia could say anything Andreas was answering for her, telling his mother, 'I'll see to that,' before placing his hand beneath Saskia's elbow and telling her in a soft voice in which she suspected only she could hear the underlying threat, 'This way, Saskia…'

CHAPTER SEVEN

'I CAN'T sleep in this room with you!'

Saskia had been able to feel herself trembling as Andreas had whisked her down a confusing maze of corridors. She had known that he must be able to feel her nervousness as well, but somehow she had managed to keep her feelings under control until they were both inside the huge elegant bedroom with the door firmly shut behind them.

Right now, though, she was in no mood to appreciate the cool elegance of her surroundings. Whirling round, she confronted Andreas determinedly. 'No way was *that* part of the deal.'

'The "deal" was that you would act as my fiancée, and that includes doing whatever has to be done to ensure that the act is believable,' he told her angrily.

'I won't sleep here with you,' Saskia protested wildly. 'I don't... I haven't...' She could hardly bear to look at the large king-sized bed as panic filled her, flooding out rationality. She had gone through so much, and now she was hot and tired and very, very afraid. Her emotions threatened to overwhelm her.

Quickly she turned away as she heard Andreas saying, almost mundanely, 'I'm going to have a shower, and if you'll take my advice you'll do the same. Then, when we're both feeling cooler and calmer, we can discuss this whole situation less emotively.'

A shower! With Andreas! Saskia stared at him in mute shocked disbelief. Did he really think that she would...that she could...?

'You can use the bathroom first,' he told her.

First! So he hadn't meant... Relief sagged through her, quickly followed by a furious burst of toxic anger.

'I don't want to use the bathroom at all,' she burst out. 'What I *want* is to be at home. My *own* home, with my own bathroom and my own bedroom. What I want is to be free of this stupid...stupid charade... What I *want*...' She had to stop as her feelings threatened to overwhelm her, but they refused to be contained, spilling out in a furious fierce torrent of angry words. 'How could you let your mother and sister think that you...that we...?' She shook her head, unable to put into words what she wanted to say.

Andreas had no such qualms.

'That we are lovers?' he supplied dramatically for her. 'What else should they think? I'm a man, Saskia, and you and I are supposed to be engaged. And if in reality we were, do you think for one minute that I wouldn't—'

'Want to test the goods before you bought them?' Saskia threw wildly at him. 'Oh, of course, a man like you would be bound to want to do that...to make sure...'

She tensed as she saw the way he was looking at her and the bitter anger in his eyes.

'That kind of comment is typical of a woman like

you,' he ground out. 'Reducing everything to terms of money. Well, let me tell you—'

But Saskia wouldn't let him finish, defending herself sharply instead as she insisted, '*You* were the one who said…'

But Andreas immediately checked her.

'What I said, or rather what I was *trying* to say before you interrupted me,' he told her grittily, 'was that if I genuinely loved you there would be no way I would be able to deny myself—or you—the pleasure of showing that love in the most intimate physical way there is. There would be no way that I could bear to let you out of my sight or my arms, certainly not for the length of a whole night.'

Saskia discovered that she had started to tremble almost violently as his words struck sharply sensitive chords deep within her body that she had not even known existed. Chords that activated a deep core of feminine longing, that brought her dangerously close to the edge of tears she had no idea why she wanted to cry. Panic raced through her veins, flooding out common sense. She could feel her heart thumping frantically with anxiety.

She opened her mouth to tell Andreas that she had changed her mind, that she wanted to go home, that she was not prepared to stay a minute longer, no matter how much he tried to blackmail her into doing so. But her panic didn't stem from any fear of him. No. It was herself she feared now, and the way she was beginning to feel, the thoughts she was beginning to have. She *couldn't* allow herself to feel that way about him. She *couldn't* be attracted to him. He wasn't her type of man at all. She abhorred the way he had treated her, the way he had misjudged her. But the shocking shaft of self-awareness, of longing she had felt as he'd described his desire for the woman he would love wasn't going to be dismissed.

'I can't...' she began, stopping as Andreas held up his hand warningly, silencing her as someone knocked on the door.

Dry-mouthed, Saskia waited whilst he went to open it, watching as their cases were brought in— not by the driver of the Land Rover but by another smaller, older man to whom Andreas was talking in Greek, smiling warmly at him as he did so, and then laughing good-humouredly as the older man looked past him at Saskia herself, before clapping him on the shoulders with a wide, beaming smile.

'What was that all about?' Saskia demanded curiously once he had gone and they were on their own again.

'Stavros was saying that it is high time I had a wife...and that I must lose no time in getting myself a fine boy child,' he added mercilessly.

Saskia could feel herself colouring to the roots of her hair as she looked everywhere but at the king-sized bed in the centre of the room.

Despite the room's air conditioning she felt stifled, unable to breathe...hunted and desperate to escape.

'I'm going to have that shower,' Andreas told her, mundanely breaking into her thoughts, turning away from her as he did so and heading for one of the three doors that opened off the bedroom.

Once he had disappeared Saskia looked at the door to the corridor, longing to have the courage to walk through it and demand that she be flown back immediately to Athens. But if she did she would lose her job—Andreas would make sure of that!

Fiercely Saskia tried to concentrate on something else, *anything* else but the appalling situation she was in. She hated what Andreas was doing to her...what he was making her do. And she hated Andreas himself too...didn't she?

Unable to answer her own question honestly, Saskia studied the view beyond the large patio doors that opened out onto an enclosed courtyard, which itself surrounded a tantalisingly tempting swimming pool complete with its own bubbling spa pool.

Small oases of green plants broke up the paving and the brilliant harshness of the sunlight. Comfortable-looking sun loungers complete with umbrellas offered a lazy way to enjoy the sunshine. The whole scene looked like something out of an exclusive holiday brochure, the kind Saskia had only been able to glance at enviously, knowing such a holiday was way beyond her means. But right now the only place she wanted to be was safe in her own home.

Andreas couldn't really expect her to share a room—never mind a bed—with him. She couldn't do it. She wouldn't...she was so...

'The bathroom's free...'

Saskia froze. She had been so engrossed in her thoughts she hadn't realised that Andreas was in the bedroom with her...standing right behind her, she recognised as she picked up the clean, warm scent of his newly showered body.

'I'll go and sort out something light for you to eat. Dinner won't be for a few hours yet, and if you'll take my advice you'll try to rest for a while. Greeks eat late and go to bed even later.'

'But I thought that we'd be having separate rooms,' Saskia burst out, unable to control her panic any longer. 'I would never have agreed to come here if I'd thought that I'd— No! Don't you dare touch me,' she protested as she felt him moving closer to her, reaching out to her. She wouldn't be able to bear it if he touched her, if he...

Frantically she turned and ran towards the door, but somehow Andreas managed to get there before her, blocking her access to it, taking hold of her, his fingers biting into the soft flesh of her arms.

'What the hell do you think you're doing?' he ground out savagely. 'What exactly is it you're pretending to be so afraid of? This? A woman like you!'

Saskia gasped and shook from head to foot as his arms closed imprisioningly around her and his mouth came down on hers. He was wearing a robe, but as she struggled to break free it was his bare skin she could feel beneath her flaying hands. Warm, damp...hard, his chest roughened by dark hairs. Her hands skittered wildly over his torso, shocked by the intimate unexpected contact with his bare skin, seeking some kind of purchase to thrust him away and finding none.

He was kissing her with an angry passion that made her feel weak, the blood roaring in her head as her brain recognised her inability to deal with the searing experience of so much furiously male arrogant sensuality.

'Stop acting like a novice, an innocent,' Saskia heard him demanding against her mouth. His tongue forced her lips to part for its entry and the hand that was imprisoning her urged her even deeper into the sensual heat of his parted thighs as he leaned back against the door, taking her with him. His free hand was on her body, arrogantly stroking its way up past her waist to the curve of her breast.

Saskia tensed in shock as it cupped her breast, his thumb-pad circling her nipple and somehow enticing it to peak into a shocking bud of delicious wanton pleasure.

She could feel the aroused heat of him like a brand, and beneath her anger she felt a sharp, spiralling stab of female curiosity and excitement...a dangerous surge to conspire with him, to allow her traitorous body to experience even more of the intimacy of their embrace.

Without knowing she had done so she opened her mouth, hesitantly allowing him access to its sweetness, shyly starting to return his kiss and even more shyly allowing her tongue to mesh seductively with his.

'Andreas? Are you in there? It's me, Athena...I need to talk to you.'

Saskia froze as she heard Athena's voice from the other side of the door, but Andreas showed no sign whatsoever of any confusion or embarrassment. Still holding Saskia against him in a grip she could not break, he opened the door and told Athena flatly, 'Not now, Athena. As you can see, Saskia and I are busy.'

'She is with *you*,' Athena snapped angrily, darting Saskia a look of icy venom. 'Why isn't she in her own room?'

'She is,' Andreas returned coolly. 'My room is Saskia's room. My bed...her bed. My body...her...'

'Your grandfather will never allow you to marry her,' Athena breathed, but Andreas was already closing the door, ignoring her insistence that he listen to her.

'Andreas, let me go,' Saskia demanded. She couldn't bear to look at him. Couldn't bear to do anything, least of all think about the way she had responded to him...the way she had encouraged him...

Derisively Andreas watched her.

'Okay, Saskia, that's enough,' he told her. 'I know I told you I wanted you to act like a faithful fiancée, but that does not mean you have to pretend to be an innocent virgin who has never—' Abruptly he stopped, frowning as he mulled over the unwanted suspicions that were striking him as he looked at Saskia's pale face and hunted eyes.

Even though he had let her go she was still shaking, trembling from head to foot, and he could have sworn just now, when he had held her in his arms and kissed her...touched her, that he was the first man to make her feel so...

For a moment he examined what he was thinking, and feeling, and then firmly dismissed his suspicions. There was no way she could be so inexperienced, no way at all. There was enough Greek in him for him to consider that the gift of her virginity, her purity, was one of the greatest gifts a woman could give to the man she loved, but his cultural heritage from his British father and schooling mocked and even deplored such archaic feelings.

Would a woman expect a man to keep himself pure until he met her? No. So why should it be any different for a woman? As a mature man he accepted and respected a woman's right to choose how she dealt with her own sexuality. But he knew too that as a lover, a husband, there would be a deeply, darkly passionate and possessive part of him that yearned to be his beloved's only partner, an ache within him to teach her, show her the delights of sensual love. And right now something about Saskia's reaction to him was sparking off a reaction he was having to fight to control, a response that was pure primitive Greek male. A need!

'I'm not sleeping in this room with you,' Saskia reiterated numbly. 'I'm…'

If she *was* acting then she deserved an Oscar, Andreas decided grimly. But a fiancée who looked terrified at the very thought of being with him was the last thing he needed. He had to calm her down, to calm them both down.

'Come with me,' he commanded, taking hold of her hand and drawing her towards one of the doors that opened off the bedroom.

When he opened it Saskia could see that the room that lay beyond it was furnished as an office, with all the latest technological equipment.

'Will it make you feel any better if I tell you that I intend to sleep in there?' Andreas demanded.

'In there? But it's an office. There's no bed,' Saskia whispered shakily.

'I can bring in one of the sun loungers and sleep on that,' Andreas told her impatiently.

'You mean it...' Saskia was wary, reluctant to trust or believe him.

Andreas nodded his head grimly, wondering why on earth he was allowing his overactive conscience to force him into such a ridiculous situation. He knew there was no way she could possibly be the naïve, frightened innocent she was behaving as though she was.

'But surely someone would notice if you removed a sun bed?' she was asking him uncertainly.

'Only my room opens out onto this pool area. It's my private territory. The main pool which everyone else uses is round the other side of the villa.'

His own private pool. Saskia fought not to be impressed, but obviously she had not fought hard enough, she recognised ruefully as Andreas gave her an impatient look.

'I'm not trying to make a point, Saskia, one-upmanship of that boastful sort is anathema to me. My grandfather may be a millionaire but I most certainly am not.'

It wasn't entirely true, but something about the look in Saskia's eyes made him want to refute any mental criticism she might have that he was some kind of idle playboy, lounging by a swimming pool all day.

'It's just that I happen to like an early-morning swim when I'm here at the villa; my sisters used to claim that I woke them up so I had this pool installed for my own use. Swimming laps helps me to clear my thoughts as well as allowing me to exercise.'

Saskia knew what he was saying, she felt the same about walking. Whenever she was worried about something, or had a problem to mull over, she walked.

As he watched her Andreas asked himself grimly why he was going to so much trouble to calm and reassure her. That frightened heartbeat he had felt thudding so anxiously against his own body just had to have been faked. There was no way it could not have been. Just like that huge-eyed watchfulness.

Saskia bit her lip as she looked away from him. It was obvious that Andreas meant what he said about sleeping in his office, but right now it wasn't their sleeping arrangements that were to the forefront of her mind so much as what was happening during their waking hours—and what she herself had just experienced when he kissed her.

She couldn't have secretly wanted him to kiss her. Surely it was impossible that that could happen without her being consciously aware of it. But what other explanation could there be for the way she had responded to him? her conscience demanded grittily.

'Right,' she could hear Andreas saying dryly, 'now that we've got *that* sorted out I've got some work to do, so why don't you have something to eat and then have a rest?'

'I need to unpack,' Saskia began to protest, but Andreas shook his head.

'One of the maids will do that for you whilst you're resting.'

When he saw her expression he told her softly, 'They work for us, Saskia. They are servants and they work to earn their living just as you and I work to earn ours.'

*   *   *

'Oh, I'm sorry, I didn't wake you, did I?' Pia said *sotto voce*. 'But it will be dinner time soon and I thought you might appreciate some extra time to get ready.'

As Saskia came fully awake and struggled to sit up in the bed she recognised that her unexpected visitor was Andreas's sister Olympia.

The arcane grin that crossed Pia's face as she added, 'We normally dress down here, not up, but Athena is bound to want to make an impact,' made Saskia warm to her friendliness.

'Where's...?' she began anxiously, but didn't get any further than the first word of her enquiry.

'Where's Andreas?' Pia supplied for her, 'Grandfather telephoned to speak to our mother and then he wanted to have a word with Andreas.' She gave a small shrug. 'He's probably still on the phone, and I have to warn you he isn't in a very good mood.' As she saw the way Saskia's eyes became watchful she hastened to assure her. 'Oh, it isn't you. It's Athena. She's brought her accountant with her and Andreas is furious. He can't stand him. None of us can, but Athena insisted that Grandfather invited Aristotle personally.'

As Pia darted about the room, switching on lamps to illuminate the darkness of the Greek evening, Saskia swung her feet to the floor. She had fallen asleep fully dressed and now she felt grubby and untidy. The thought of having to sit down at a dinner table with Andreas and Athena was not one she was looking forward to, but Pia was right about one thing: she *would* need to make an impact. Andreas would no doubt expect it of her. Still, with her suitcase full of the new clothes he had insisted on buying for her, she had no excuse *not* to do so.

'Maria's already unpacked your cases for you,' Pia informed her. 'I helped her,' she added. 'I love that little black number you've brought with you. It's to die for. Your clothes are gorgeous. Andreas kept coming in and telling me not to make so much noise in case I woke you up.' She pulled another face. 'He's so protective of you.

'Mama and I are so glad that he's met you,' she added more quietly, giving Saskia a look of warm confidence that immediately made her feel horribly guilty. 'We both love him to bits, of course,' she went on, 'and that hardly makes us impartial. But we were beginning to get so afraid that he might just give in to Grandfather and Athena for Grandfather's sake—and we both know he could *never* love her. I suppose he's told you about what she did when he was younger?'

Without waiting for Saskia to say anything Pia continued in a quick burst of flurried words, 'I'm not supposed to know about it really. Lydia, my sister, told me, and swore me to secrecy, but of course it's all right to discuss it with you because Andreas must have told you about it. He was only fifteen at the time—just a boy, really—and she was *so* much older and on the point of getting married. I know the actual age gap in terms of years would be nothing if it had been between two adults, but Andreas wasn't an adult. He was still at school and she... I think it was wonderfully brave and moral of Andreas to refuse to go to bed with her—and do you know something else? I think that although Athena *claims* to love him a part of her really wants to punish him for not letting her—well, you know!'

Athena had tried to *seduce* Andreas when he had still been a schoolboy! Saskia had to fight hard to control both her shock and the distaste Pia's revelations were causing her.

It was true that in terms of years—a mere seven or so—the age gap between them was not large. But for a woman in her twenties to attempt to seduce a boy of fifteen—surely that was almost sexual abuse? A cold shiver touched Saskia's skin, icy fingers spreading a chilling message through her.

Would a woman who was prepared to do something like that allow a mere bogus fiancée to come between her and the man she wanted? And Athena obviously did want Andreas very badly indeed— even if her motivation for doing so was shrouded in secrecy.

Andreas was such a very *male* man it was hard to imagine him in the role of hunted rather than hunter. If ever a man had been designed by nature to be proactive, arrogant and predatory that man was, in Saskia's opinion, Andreas. But there was something so alien to Saskia's own experience in Athena, a coldness, a greed, almost an obsessiveness that Saskia found it hard to relate to her or even think of her in terms of being a member of her own sex.

Her determination to marry Andreas was chillingly formidable.

'Of course, if it wasn't for Grandfather's health there wouldn't be any problem,' Pia was saying ruefully. 'We all know that. Grandfather likes to think that because he works for him Andreas is financially dependent on him, but…' She stopped, shaking her head.

'You are going to wear the black, aren't you? I'm dying to see you in it. You've got the colouring for it. I look so drab in black, although you can bet that Athena will wear it. Whoops!' She grimaced as they both heard male footsteps in the corridor outside the bedroom. 'That will be Andreas, and he'll scalp me if he thinks I'm being a pest.'

Saskia tensed as Andreas came into the room, watching as his glance went from the bed to where she was standing in the corner of the room.

'Pia,' he began ominously, 'I told you…'

'I was awake when she came,' Saskia intervened protectively. She liked Andreas's sister, and if she'd been genuinely in love with him and planning to marry him she knew she would have been delighted to have found a potential friend in this warm-hearted, impulsive woman.

Pia launched herself at Andreas, laughing up into his face as she hugged him and told him triumphantly, 'See? You are wrong, big brother, and you must not be so firm and bossy with me otherwise Saskia will not want to marry you. And now that I have met her I am determined that she will be my sister-in-law. We were just discussing what she is going to wear for dinner,' she added. 'I have warned her that Athena will be dressed to kill!'

'If you don't take yourself off to your own room so that we can *all* get ready, Athena is going to be the only one who is dressed for anything,' Andreas told her dryly.

Kissing his forehead, Pia released him and hurried

to the door, pausing as she opened it to give Saskia an impish grin and remind her, 'Wear the black!'

'I'm sorry,' Andreas apologised after the door had closed behind her. 'I asked her not to disturb you.'

So he hadn't been deceived by her fib, Saskia recognised.

'I don't mind; I like her,' Saskia responded, this time telling him the truth.

'Mmm... Pia's likeability is something I'm afraid she tends to trade on on occasion. As the baby of the family she's a past mistress at getting her own way,' he told Saskia in faint exasperation, before glancing at his watch and informing her, 'You've got half an hour to get ready.'

Saskia took a deep steadying breath. Something about the revelations Pia had made had activated the deep core of sympathy for others that was so much a part of her nature. Somewhere deep inside her a switch had been thrown, a sea change made, and without her knowing quite how it had happened Andreas had undergone a transformation, from her oppressor and a dictator whom she loathed and feared to someone who deserved her championship and help. She had a role which she was now determined she was going to play to the very best of her ability.

'Half an hour,' she repeated in as businesslike a manner as she could. 'Then in that case I should like to use the bathroom first.'

CHAPTER EIGHT

'So, Saskia, how do you think you will adjust to being a Greek wife—if you and Andreas *do* actually get married?'

Saskia could hear Pia's indrawn gasp of indignation at the way Athena had framed her question, but she refused to allow herself to be intimidated by the other woman. Ever since they had all taken their places at the dinner table Saskia had recognised that Athena was determined to unnerve and upset her as much as she could. However, before she could say anything Andreas was answering the question for her.

'There is no "if" about it Athena,' he told her implacably. 'Saskia *will* become my wife.'

Now it was Saskia's turn to stifle her own potentially betraying gasp of shock, but she couldn't control her instinctive urge to look anxiously across the table at Andreas. What would he do when he ultimately had to back down and admit to Athena that their engagement was over? That was *his* problem and not hers, she tried to remind herself steadily.

Something odd had happened to her somehow; she was convinced of it. Andreas had walked out of the office adjoining 'their' bedroom earlier this evening and come to a standstill in front of her, saying quietly, 'I doubt that any man looking at you now could do anything other than wish that you were his, Saskia.'

She had certainly never had any desire to go on the stage—far from it—and yet from that moment she had felt as though somehow she had stepped into a new persona. Suddenly she had become Andreas's fiancée and, like any woman in love, not only was she proud to be with the man she loved, she also felt very femalely protective of him. The anxiety in her eyes now was *for* him and *because* of him. How would he feel when Athena tauntingly threw the comment he had just made back in his face? How must he have felt when he had first realised, as a boy, just what she wanted from him?

'Wives. I love wives.' Aristotle, Athena's accountant, grinned salaciously, leaning towards Saskia so that he could put his hand on her arm.

Immediately she turned away from him. Saskia fully shared Pia's view of Athena's accountant. Although he was quite tall, the heavy, weighty structure of his torso made him look almost squat. His thick black hair was heavily oiled and the white suit he was wearing over a black shirt, in Saskia's opinion at least, did him no favours. Andreas, on the other hand, looked sexily cool and relaxed in elegantly tailored trousers with a cool white cotton shirt.

If she had privately thought her black dress might be rather over the top she had swiftly realised how right Pia had been to suggest that she wore it once she had seen Athena's outfit.

Her slinky skintight white dress left nothing to the imagination.

'It was designed especially for me,' Saskia had heard her smirking to Andreas. 'And it is made to be worn exactly the way I most love—next to my skin,' she had added, loudly enough for Saskia to overhear. 'Which reminds me. I hope you have warned your fiancée that I like to share your morning swim so she won't be too shocked...' She had turned to Saskia. 'Andreas is like me, he likes to swim best in his skin,' she had told her purringly.

In his skin. Saskia hadn't been able to prevent herself from giving Andreas a brief shocked look which, fortunately, Athena had put down to Saskia's jealousy at the thought of another woman swimming nude with her fiancée.

Whilst Saskia had been digesting this stomach-churning disclosure she had heard Andreas himself replying brusquely, 'I can only recall one occasion on which you attempted to join me in my morning lap session, Athena, and I recall too that I told you then how little I appreciate having my morning peace interrupted.'

'Oh, dear.' Athena had pouted, unabashed. 'Are you afraid that I have said something you didn't want your fiancée to know? But surely, Andreas,' she had murmured huskily, reaching out to place her hand on his arm, 'she *must* realise that a man as attractive as you...as virile as you...will have had other lovers before her...'

Her brazenness had almost taken Saskia's breath away. She could imagine just how she would be feeling right now if Andreas *had* indeed been her fiancée. How jealous and insecure Athena's words would be making her feel. No woman wanted to be reminded of the other women who had shared an intimate relationship with her beloved before her.

But Andreas, it seemed, was completely unfazed

by Athena's revelations. He had simply removed her arm by the expedient of stepping back from her and putting his own arm around Saskia's shoulders. He had drawn her so close to his body that Saskia had known he must be able to feel the fine tremor of reaction she was unable to suppress. A tremor which had increased to a full-flooded convulsion when his lean fingers had started almost absently to caress the smooth ball of her bare shoulder.

'Saskia knows that she is the only woman I have ever loved—the woman I want to spend my life with.'

The more she listened to and watched Athena the more Saskia subscribed to Pia's belief that it wasn't love that was motivating the other woman. Sometimes she looked at Andreas as though she hated him and wanted to totally destroy him.

Aristotle, or 'Ari' as he had told Saskia he preferred to be called, was still trying to engage her attention, but she was deliberately trying to feign a lack of awareness of that fact. There was something about him she found so loathsome that the thought of even the hot damp touch of his hand on her arm made her shudder with distaste. However, good manners forced her to respond to his questions as politely as she could, even when she thought they were intolerable and intrusive. He had already told her that were he Andreas's accountant he would be insisting she sign a prenuptial contract to make sure that if the marriage ended Andreas's money would be safe.

Much to Saskia's surprise Andreas himself had thoroughly confounded her by joining in the conversation and telling Aristotle grimly that he would never ask the woman he loved to sign such an agreement.

'Money is nothing when compared with love,' he had told Aristotle firmly in a deep, implacable voice, his words so obviously genuine that Saskia had found she was holding her breath a little as she listened to him.

Then he had looked at her, and Saskia had remembered just how *they* had met and what he really thought of her, and suddenly she had felt the most bitter taste of despair in her mouth and she had longed to tell him how wrong he was.

At least she had the comfort of knowing that his mother and sister liked her, and Pia had assured her that their elder sister was equally pleased that Andreas had fallen in love, and was looking forward to meeting Saskia when she and her husband and their children came to the island later in the month.

'Lydia's husband is a diplomat, and they are in Brussels at the moment, but she is longing to meet you,' Pia had told her.

She would have hated it if Andreas's close family had *not* liked and welcomed her.

Abruptly Saskia felt her face start to burn. What on earth was she thinking? She was only *playing* the part of Andreas's fiancée. Their engagement was a fiction, a charade...a *lie* created simply to help him escape from the trap that Athena was trying to set for him. What she must not forget was that it was a lie he had tricked and blackmailed her into colluding with.

Aristotle was saying something to her about wanting to show her the villa's gardens. Automatically

Saskia shook her head, her face burning with fresh colour as she saw the way Andreas was watching her, a mixture of anger and warning in his eyes. He couldn't seriously think she would actually *accept* Aristotle's invitation?

'Saskia has had a long day. I think it's time we said our goodnights,' she heard him saying abruptly as he stood up.

Saskia looked quickly round the table. It was obvious from the expressions of everyone else just what interpretation they were putting on Andreas's decision, and Saskia knew that the heat washing her face and throat could only confirm their suspicions.

'Andreas…' she started to protest as he came round to her chair and stood behind her. 'I don't…'

'You're wasting your breath, Saskia.' Pia chuckled. 'Because my dear brother obviously *does*! Oh, you needn't put that lordly expression on for me, brother dear.' She laughed again, before adding mischievously, 'And I wouldn't mind betting that you won't be lapping the pool at dawn…'

'Pia!' her mother protested, pink-cheeked, whilst Athena gave Saskia a look of concentrated hatred.

Hastily Saskia stood up, and then froze as Aristotle did the same, insisting in a thick voice, 'I must claim the privilege of family friend and kiss the new addition to the family goodnight.'

Before Saskia could evade him he was reaching for her, but before he could put his words into action Andreas was standing between them, announcing grimly, 'There is only one man *my* fiancée kisses…'

'If you'll take my advice, you'll keep well away from Aristotle. He has a very unsavoury reputation with women. His ex-wife has accused him of being violent towards her and—'

Saskia turned as she stepped into the bedroom, her anger showing. 'You can't mean what I *think* you mean,' she demanded whilst Andreas closed the door. How could he possibly imagine that she would even contemplate being interested in a man like the accountant? It was an insult she was simply not prepared to tolerate.

'Can't I?' Andreas countered curtly. 'You're here for one reason and one reason only, Saskia. You're here to act as my fiancée. Whilst I can appreciate that, being the woman you are, the temptation to feather your nest a little and do what you so obviously do best must be a strong one, let me warn you now against giving in to it. If you do, in fact...'

If she *did*... Why, she would rather *die* than let a slimeball like Ari come anywhere near her, Saskia reflected furiously. And to think that back there in the dining room she had *actually* felt sympathetic towards Andreas, had actually wanted to *protect* him. Now, though, her anger shocked through her in a fierce, dangerous flood of pride.

'If you want the truth, I find Ari almost as repulsively loathsome as I do you,' she threw bitterly at him.

'You dare to speak of me in the same breath as that reptile? How dare you speak so of me...or to me...?' Andreas demanded, his anger surging to match hers as he reached out to grab hold of her. His eyes smouldered with an intensity of emotion that Saskia could see was threatening to get out of control.

'That man is an animal—worse than an animal. Only last year he narrowly escaped standing on a criminal charge. I cannot understand why Athena tolerates him and I have told her so.'

'Perhaps she wants to make you jealous.'

It was an off-the-cuff remark, full of bravado, but Saskia wished immediately she had not said it when she saw the way the smoulder suddenly became a savage flare of fury.

'*She* does? Or *you* do...? Oh, yes, I saw the way he was looking at you over dinner...touching you...'

'That was nothing to do with me,' Saskia protested, but she could sense that the words hadn't touched him, that something else was fuelling his anger and feeding it, something that was hidden from her but which Andreas himself obviously found intolerable.

'And as for you finding me *loathsome*,' Andreas said through gritted teeth. 'Perhaps it is unchivalrous, *ungentlemanly* of me to say so, but that wasn't loathing I could see in your eyes earlier on today. It wasn't *loathing* I could hear in your voice, *feel* in your body...was it? *Was it?*' he demanded sharply.

Saskia started to tremble.

'I don't know,' she fibbed wildly. 'I can't remember.'

It was, she recognised a few seconds later, the worst possible thing she could have said. Because immediately Andreas pounced, whispering with soft savagery, 'No? Then perhaps I should help you to remember...'

She heard herself starting to protest, but somehow the words were lost—not because Andreas was refusing to listen, but because her lips were refusing to speak.

'So when exactly *was* it that you found me so loathsome Saskia?' Andreas was demanding as he closed both his arms around her, forming them into a prison from which it was impossible for her to escape. 'When I did this…?' His mouth was feathering over hers, teasing and tantalising it, arousing a hot torrent of sensation she didn't want to experience. 'Or when I did *this*…?'

Now his tongue-tip was probing the lips she was trying so desperately to keep firmly closed, stroking them, tracing their soft curves, over and over again, until she could hear herself moaning helplessly as they parted softly for him. But still it seemed he hadn't extracted his pound of flesh, because even this victory wasn't enough for him.

'What? Still no answer…? I wonder why not,' he was taunting her, before adding bitingly, 'Or do I need to wonder at all? You are a woman who is used to giving her body to a man, Saskia, who is used to experiencing pleasure. And right now you want that pleasure from *me*.'

'No,' Saskia moaned in denial, trying to turn her face away from his and to break free of him.

'Yes,' he insisted rawly. '*Yes*. Admit it, Saskia… You *want* me… Your body wants *mine*. It wants the sexual satisfaction it's used to…it aches and craves for.'

A shudder of shock ripped through her as Saskia recognised the truth of what he was saying. She *did* want him, but not in the way he was suggesting. She wanted him as a woman wanted the man she loved, she realised shakily. She wanted him as her lover, not merely as her sexual partner, someone with whom she could find a release for a basic physical need, as he was so cruelly saying. But how could she love him? She *couldn't*... But she *did*.

She had fallen in love with him virtually the moment she had set eyes on him, Saskia acknowledged despairingly, but she had told herself that because of her loyalty to her friend he was out of bounds to her and that she could not, *must* not allow herself to have such feelings, just as she could not allow herself to have them now. Although for very different reasons. Megan was no longer a barrier to her loving Andreas, but Andreas himself and what he thought about her certainly was.

'Let me go, Andreas,' she demanded.

'Not until you have admitted that I am right and that you want me,' Andreas refused. 'Or are you trying to goad me into *proving* to you that I am right?'

Saskia flinched as she felt the suffocating, dangerously toxic mix of fear and excitement explode inside her.

She hesitated whilst she tried to formulate the right response, the only sane, sensible response she could give, and then she realised that she had waited too long as Andreas told her rawly, 'You've pushed me too far, Saskia. I want you, but you already know that, don't you? How could a woman like you *not* know it? You can feel it in my body, can't you?' he demanded. 'Here...'

Helplessly Saskia leaned against him whilst she tried to absorb the shock of having her hand taken and placed so explicitly against the hard, intimate throb of his maleness. If only she could find the strength to drag her hand away, to tell him that she didn't want the intimacy he was forcing on her. But despairingly she knew that she was too weak, that there was no way she could stop herself from aching to use the opportunity he had given her to touch and explore him, to know him…to know his maleness…to—

She gave a small moan as her body started to shake with tremors of desire. Andreas's heart was pounding so savagely that she could feel it almost inside her own body. Earlier in the evening, when he had almost absently caressed the ball of her shoulder—the touch of an established lover for his beloved—she had shuddered in mute delight, but that was nothing to what she was feeling now.

She ached for him, hungered for him, and when she closed her eyes she could see him as Athena had so tauntingly described him—proud and naked as his body sliced the water. She moaned again, a high, sharp sound this time that had Andreas covering her mouth with the hard, hot, demanding pressure of his, the words he was groaning against her lost as his passion sent a kick of shocking voluptuous pleasure searing through her.

Her mouth was properly open beneath his now, her tongue hungry for the sensual melding stroke of his, and the intensity of her own feelings was dizzying and dazzling her.

'You want me… You need me…'

She could feel him mouthing the words and she couldn't deny them, her body, her emotions were saturated with the intensity of a response to him so new to her that she had no defences against it.

Everything else was suddenly forgotten, unimportant. Everything else and every*one* else. All she needed... All she wanted... All she could ever want was here within her reach.

She moaned and trembled as she felt Andreas's hands on her body and over her dress, their touch hard, hungry...excitingly, *dangerously* male. The unfamiliar intimacy of his body against hers was depriving her of the ability to think or to reason properly. There was no place for reason to exist in this new world she was inhabiting anyway.

'I want to see you...watch you whilst I make love to you,' Andreas was saying thickly to her. 'I want *you* to see me... My God, but I can understand *now* just why all those other men fell victim to you. There's something about you, some witchery, some— What's wrong?' he demanded as he felt the abrupt way Saskia had tensed against him in rejection.

Saskia could not bear to look at him.

With those few contemptuous words he had destroyed everything, totally obliterated her wonderful new world and brought her crashing back to her old one. She felt sick to her soul from her own behaviour, her own folly.

'No, no, I don't want *this*,' she protested frantically, pushing Andreas away.

'What the...?' She could hear the anger in his voice, feel it almost, but still he released her.

'If this is some kind of game—' he began to warn her, and then stopped, shaking his head in disbelief.

'My God, I must have been out of my mind anyway, to even contemplate… I suppose that's what too many years of celibacy does for a man,' he threw at her unkindly. 'I never thought I'd be idiotic enough…'

He turned back to her, stopping when Saskia froze.

'You're quite safe,' he told her grimly. 'I'm not going to touch you. There's no way—' He broke off and shook his head again, and then walked abruptly away from her, telling her brusquely, 'I've got some work to do.'

The bedroom was in darkness when Saskia woke up, and at first she didn't know what had woken her. Then she heard it again, the rhythmic sound of someone swimming. The patio doors to the pool area were open, and as she turned her head to look towards them she could see the discreet lights which were illuminating it.

Andreas was swimming… She looked at her watch. It was three o'clock in the morning and Andreas was swimming…tirelessly up and down the pool. Warily she sat up in bed to get a closer look as his powerful crawl took him to the far side of the pool. As he executed his turn Saskia lay down again. She didn't want him to see her watching him.

Beneath the bedclothes she was naked, apart from a tiny pair of briefs. The one thing Andreas had apparently forgotten to buy for her had turned out to be any kind of nightwear. *That* discovery had caused her to remain for nearly fifteen minutes in the locked privacy of the bathroom, agonising over what she should do until she had finally found the courage to

open the door and make an undignified bolt for the
bed, her body hidden from view by the towel she
had wrapped around it. Not that she need have been
so concerned. Andreas had remained out of sight in
his office.

But he wasn't in his office now. Now he was
swimming in the pool.

Beneath the protective cover of the bedclothes
Saskia's brain worked feverishly. Should he be
swimming alone at night? Was it safe? What if...?
Almost the very second that fear formed her ears
registered the fact that she could no longer hear the
sound of Andreas swimming. Quickly she lowered
the bedclothes and looked anxiously towards the pool
area. The water was still, calm—and empty of its sole
swimmer.

Andreas! Where—? She gripped hold of the bedclothes as she saw him climbing out of the water—
totally naked—totally! She tried to drag her recalci-
trant gaze away from his body but it was no use; it
was refusing to listen to her, refusing to obey her,
remaining fixed in hungry female appreciation on the
pagan male beauty of Andreas's nakedness.

Surely any woman would have found the sight of
Andreas breathtaking, Saskia thought fervently, her
gaze devouring the pure sensuality of his back view
as he walked across the tiles. His skin shone sleekly,
still damp from his swim, and beneath it the muscles
moved in a way that had a shockingly disconcerting
effect on her *own* body.

Naively Saskia had always previously assumed
that there could be little difference in seeing a statue
or a painting of a naked man and viewing the real

thing, but now she knew how wrong she had been. Perhaps it was her love for him that made the difference, perhaps it was... She gasped as he suddenly turned round. He seemed to be looking right into the bedroom. Could he see her? Did he *know* that she was watching him? She lay perfectly still, praying that he could not do so, unable to bear the humiliation of his mockery if he were to come in to her now. If he were to...

She just managed to suppress the audible sound of her own longing. If he came to her now and held her, touched her, kissed her...*took* her as she was so aching for him to do, it wouldn't be in love but in lust. Was that really what she wanted? she asked herself sternly. No, of course it wasn't, was her helpless response. What she wanted was for Andreas to love her the way she did him.

He was turning away from her now, his body silhouetted by the light. Saskia sucked in her breath sharply, every feminine instinct and desire she possessed flagrantly ignoring her attempts to control them. He looked... He was... He was *perfect* she acknowledged, silently whispering the soft accolade beneath her breath as her eyes rounded and she saw that the male reality of him far, far outreached anything she had ever thought of in her innocent virginal imaginings.

Once again he looked towards the bedroom and Saskia held her breath, praying...hoping...*waiting*... She expelled it on a small rush of sound as he reached down and retrieved his robe, shrugging it on before walking not back to the bedroom and to her but away from it. Where was he going? she wondered. Back to his office?

For what felt like a long time after he had gone Saskia lay where she was, afraid to move, unable to sleep and even more afraid to think. What was the matter with her? How could she possibly love a man who had treated her as Andreas had done, who had blackmailed her, threatened her, refused to allow her to tell him the truth about herself? A man who had the lowest possible opinion of her and yet who, despite that, had still kissed her. How could she? Saskia closed her eyes. She didn't know the answer to that question. All she knew was that her emotions, her heart, her deepest self were crying out—how could she *not* love him?

'Sunbathing? I never thought I'd see the day when you would just laze around,' Pia teased Andreas as she came hurrying out of the villa in the tiniest little bikini Saskia had ever seen and curled up on the vacant sun bed next to where Saskia was lying.

'Saskia didn't have a good night. She needs to rest and I didn't want her overdoing things or lying too long in our strong sun,' Andreas lied unblushingly to his sister.

'Oh, poor you,' Pia immediately sympathised with Saskia as she studied her pale face.

Guiltily Saskia said nothing. After all, she could hardly admit that the reason she was so jaded was because she had spent so many of the night hours when she should have been sleeping thinking about, *fantasising* about the man lying right next to her. In daylight Saskia dared not recall the very personal and intimate nature of her fantasies. She knew that if she did so her face would be as brightly coloured as it was now pale. Mercifully Andreas had put her huge eyes and pale face down to travel tiredness.

'Well, that's one improvement you've made on my brother's lifestyle already, Saskia,' Pia approved with a grin. 'Normally when he comes to the villa we can't get him out of the office. When did Grandfather say he is going to arrive?' she asked Andreas.

'I must say I'm surprised that your grandfather intends to come to the island at all at the moment,' Athena answered for Andreas as she and her accountant came out of the villa to join them.

Saskia's heart sank a little as she saw them. Over breakfast Ari had been so over-fulsome in his praise of her, and so obviously sexually motivated, that she had been glad to escape from him.

As Pia started to frown Athena added maliciously, 'He isn't very happy with you right now, Andreas…'

'My grandfather is never happy with anyone who takes a different view from his,' Andreas told her dryly. 'He has a quick temper and a short fuse and thankfully an even shorter memory—'

Andreas had insisted that Saskia was to lie beneath the protection of a sun umbrella because of her fair skin, but as she watched Athena untying the wrap she was wearing to reveal an even smaller bikini than Pia's, Saskia felt envious of her rich golden tan.

'How uncomfortable you must be lying in the shade,' Athena said, adding bitchily, 'I would *hate* to have such a pale skin. It always looks so…'

'Saskia's skin reminds *me* of the purest alabaster,' Andreas interrupted Athena smoothly.

'Alabaster—oh, but that is so cold.' Athena

smiled, giving Saskia an assessing look. 'Oh, now you are frowning and looking grumpy,' she told Andreas softly, 'and I know *just* the cure for that. Let me put some oil on for you, Andreas, and then...'

Saskia could hardly believe it when she heard herself saying firmly, 'I'll do that for you, darling.' Turning to look at Athena, she added boldly, 'A fiancée's privilege.' And then, ignoring both the frowning look Andreas was giving her and her own shaking hands, she got up off her sun lounger, took the bottle of oil Pia was offering her with an approving smile and walked over to where Andreas was lying.

Very carefully Saskia poured a little of the oil into her cupped hand and then, even more carefully, leaned over Andreas's prone body, making sure as she did so that she stood between his sun bed and the one Athena was reclining on in a pose carefully designed to flaunt to full effect her generous breasts.

Saskia's hair swung over her face as she nervously started to smooth the oil over Andreas shoulders. His skin felt warm and sleek beneath her touch. As sleek as it had looked last night. She paused as her hands began to tremble. Last night! She must *not* think about *that* now. But somehow she found herself doing so; somehow, too, her hands were moving sensually against his skin, stroking, smoothing, even kneading instinctively when she found that his muscles were bunching beneath her touch.

He had been lying on his stomach with his eyes closed, but suddenly they opened and he told her abruptly, 'That's enough. I was about to go for a swim anyway.'

Even so it was still several seconds before he actually got up and walked away from her to the end of the pool, diving in cleanly and then swimming virtually a full length beneath the water before resurfacing and starting to lap the pool with a hard, fast-paced crawl.

Andreas tried to concentrate on what he was doing, to empty his head of any thoughts as he always did when he was swimming. It was his favourite way of relaxing—or at least it had been. Right now the *last* thing he felt was relaxed. Even without closing his eyes he could still remember exactly how it had felt to have Saskia's hands moving over his body, soft, caressing…knowing…

He slid beneath the water, swimming under it as he tried to control his aching body. God, but he wanted her; ached for her; lusted for her. He had *never* felt like this about anyone before, never needed anyone with such an intensity, never been in a situation where he simply could not control himself either physically or emotionally. She *must* know what she was doing to him, a woman of *her* experience…a woman who prowled bars at night looking for a man. Of *course* she must; of course she *did*. And yet…

And yet he couldn't stop himself from contrasting what he knew cerebrally about her with the way she had felt in his arms, the soft, hot sweetness of her kiss, the desire hazing her eyes and the shock which had later replaced it. She had caught him off guard just now, when she had refused to allow Athena to touch him—caught him off guard and filled him with a certain hot male triumph and pride that she should feel so possessive about him. But of course she didn't—did she? She was simply acting, playing out the role he had forced her into.

Andreas frowned. His own mental use of the word 'forced' and the admission which it brought rasped against his conscience like sandpaper. It was wholly out of character for him, against his strongest held beliefs to force anyone to do anything, but he had begun to fear he could find no way out of the present situation without endangering his grandfather's health. What he was offering was an explanation, not an excuse, he warned himself sternly and if he had now discovered that he had merely exchanged one hazard for another which was even more potentially dangerous then he had no one but himself to blame.

Had Saskia seen that betraying surge of his body before he had turned away from her? Athena had. Athena... Andreas's mouth hardened.

At fifteen, and still a schoolboy, he had tried to convince himself that he was mature enough to take over his father's role, strong enough to support and protect his mother and his sisters. But a part of him had still been childish and he had often ended up crying alone at night in his bed, confused and angry and missing his father, wondering furiously why he had had to die.

That period had surely been the worst of his life: the loss of his father and then Athena's attempt to seduce him. Two events which together had propelled him into an adulthood and maturity he had in no way been prepared for.

Athena's desire for him had held none of the classic 'Mrs Robinson' allure. She had been coming on to him for weeks, ever since he had returned home from school for the summer holidays, but he had never dreamed that she was doing anything other than playing some mysterious adult female game that was beyond his ability to comprehend—until the day he had found her in his room—naked!

When she had handed him the vibrator she was stroking herself with, commanding him to use it on her, it had been all he could do not to turn on his heels and run. But boys ran, and he hadn't wanted to be a boy, but a man...the man his father would have wanted him to be, the man his mother and sisters needed him to be.

'I don't think you should be in here, do you?' he had asked her woodenly, avoiding looking at her naked body. 'You are engaged to be married.'

She had laughed at him then, but she hadn't been laughing later, when he had held open his bedroom door and commanded her to leave, warning her that if she didn't he would have no compunction in getting a couple of members of staff to physically remove her.

She had gone, but not immediately, not until she had tried to change his mind.

'You have a man's body,' she had told him angrily. 'But like a fool you have no knowledge of what to do with it. Why won't you let me show you?' she had coaxed. 'What is it you are so afraid of?'

'I'm not afraid,' he had responded stoically, and truthfully. It hadn't been fear that had stopped him from taking advantage of what she was offering but anger and loathing.

But Athena was a woman who couldn't endure to accept that he didn't want her. Tough! Her feelings, if she genuinely had any—which he personally doubted—were her problem. His grandfather was a very different matter, though, and even without the cloud currently hanging over his health, Andreas would have been reluctant to quarrel with him—though he felt that the old man was being both stubborn and difficult. How much of the blame for that lay with Athena and how much with his grandfather's fiercely guarded fear of growing old and the future Andreas could only hazard a guess at.

It was ironic, really, that the means he had adopted to help him overcome his problems should have resulted in causing him even more. An example, perhaps, of the modern-day ethos behind the ancient Greek mythology Saskia had expressed a love of. She might love Greek mythology but she most certainly did not love him. Andreas frowned, not wanting to pursue such a line of thought.

'That is a very pretty little ring you are wearing,' Athena commented disparagingly as she got up off the lounger and came to stand next to Saskia.

They were alone at the poolside, Athena's accountant having gone to make some telephone calls and Pia having left to help her mother, who was preparing for the arrival of her father.

'But an engagement ring is no guarantee of marriage,' Athena continued. 'You look like a sensible girl to me, Saskia. Andreas is a very wealthy and experienced man. Men like him get so easily bored. You must know that yourself. I suspect that the chances of you actually walking down the aisle and marrying Andreas are very limited indeed, and they will become even more slender once Andreas's grandfather arrives. He doesn't want Andreas to marry you. He is very old-fashioned and very Greek. He has other plans for his only grandson and for the future of the business he has built up.'

She paused, watching Saskia calculatingly, and Saskia knew what she was thinking. Athena too had other plans for Andreas's future.

'If you really loved Andreas then surely *he* would be far more important to you than your own feelings. Andreas is devoted to his grandfather. Oh, I know he may not show it, but I can promise you that he is. Think what it would do to him emotionally, not to mention financially, if there were to be a rift between them. Andreas's mother and his sisters are both financially dependent on their grandfather... If he were to banish Andreas from his life then Andreas would be banished from *their* lives as well.'

Athena gave a deep, theatrical sigh and then asked pseudo-gently, 'How long do you think he would continue to want *you* once that had happened? And I can *make* it happen, Saskia...you know that, don't you. His grandfather listens to me. It is because he wants my business to be joined to his, of course. That is the Greek way of doing things.' She bared her teeth and gave Saskia an unkind smile. 'It is *not* the Greek way of doing things for a millionaire to allow his heir to marry a penniless foreigner.

'But let's talk of something more pleasant. There is no reason why we shouldn't come to a mutually happy arrangement—you and I. I *could* sit back and wait for Andreas to leave you, but I will be honest with you. I am approaching the age when it may become less easy for me to give Andreas the sons he will want. So, to make it easy for us both, I have a proposition to put to you. I am willing to pay you *one million pounds* to remove you from Andreas's life—permanently.'

Saskia could feel the blood draining out of her face as shock hit her. Somehow she managed to drag herself into a sitting position on the sun lounger and then to stand up, so that she and Athena were face to face.

'Money can't buy love,' she told her fiercely. 'And it can't buy me. Not one million pounds, not one hundred million pounds! *No* amount.' Tears stung her eyes and she told herself that shock had put them there. 'If at any time Andreas wants to end our engagement then that is his prerogative, but—'

'You're a fool—do you know that?' Athena breathed, her whole face contorted with fury and malice. 'Do you really think Andreas meant what he said about not insisting on a prenuptial agreement? Ha! His grandfather will *make* him have you sign one, and when Andreas grows tired of you, as he undoubtedly will, you will get *nothing*...not even any child he may have given you. Greek men do not give up their children. Greek *families* do not give up their heirs.'

Saskia didn't want to hear any more. Without even bothering to pick up her wrap she started to walk towards the house, only just managing to prevent herself from breaking into a run.

As Saskia reached the house Pia was coming out of it through the open patio door.

'Saskia...' she began in concern, but Saskia shook

her head, knowing she was in no fit state to talk to her—to her or indeed to anyone. She felt degraded by what Athena had said to her, degraded and angry. How dared Athena believe that her love was for sale...that *money* mattered more to her than Andreas...that she would *ever*...? Abruptly Saskia stopped. What was she *thinking*? She turned round and went back outside, heading not for the pool area but beyond it...to the island and the pathway along the cliffs. She needed to be on her own.

The full irony of what had happened was only just beginning to sink in. She had agreed to come to the island only because Andreas had blackmailed her into doing so and because she couldn't afford to lose the income from her job. Yet when she was offered what amounted to financial security for life, not just for herself but more importantly for her beloved grandmother, as well as an immediate escape from her intolerable situation, she turned both down.

Angrily Pia started to hurry towards where Athena was lying sunning herself. After what she had just overheard there was no way she was not going to tell Athena what she thought of her. How dared she treat Saskia like that, trying to bribe her into leaving Andreas?

Andreas!

Pia came to an abrupt halt. Perhaps she ought to tell her brother what Athena had been up to and let him deal with her. Saskia had looked so dreadfully upset, and no wonder. Reluctantly Pia listened to the inner voice warning her that Andreas would not thank her for pre-empting his right to be the one to confront Athena. Turning on her heel, she walked back inside the villa in search of Andreas.

CHAPTER NINE

LESS than a third of the way along the path that cir-
cumnavigated the island Saskia stopped walking and
turned round. She couldn't go on; she had had
enough. Loving Andreas—being so close to him every
day in one sense and yet with such an unbridgeable
gap between them in all the senses that really mattered—was more than she could cope with. Her love
for him, her longing for him, was tearing her apart.

Slowly she started to walk back to the villa. She
had no idea what she was going to do—throw herself
on Andreas's mercy and beg him to release her from
their 'agreement'? There was no point in trying to
tell him what Athena had done. He was hardly likely
to believe her, not with his opinion of her, and besides, she didn't want him to know. If he did...once
he did... Andreas was no fool, he was an astute,
sharp-minded businessman, it wouldn't take him
long to guess what had happened, how she felt, and
that was something she could not endure.

Once she reached the villa Saskia went straight to
'her' room which, thankfully, was empty. The maid
had been in and the bed was freshly made. Quickly
removing her swimsuit, she went to have a shower.

'Andreas,' Athena purred seductively as she saw him
coming out of his grandfather's office.

'Not now, Athena.' Andreas cut her short. He had spent the best part of the last couple of hours trying to come to terms with feelings he had never expected to have, never mind *wanted* to have, and now that he had come to a decision he was anxious to act on it without any delay, especially from Athena.

It was no use trying to hide the truth from himself any longer.

He had fallen in love with Saskia. How? Why? When? To his exasperation no amount of analytical self-probing on his part had been able to produce any kind of logical answers to such questions. All his heart, his body, his emotions, his very soul kept insisting over and over again was they wanted her; loved her; craved and needed her. If the logical-thinking part of him that was already fighting a desperate rearguard action should dare to argue, then his emotions would see to it that his life was no longer worth living.

But look at what she *is* he had tried to remind himself. But his emotions had refused to listen. He loved her as she was, past errors of judgement and all. Errors of *judgement*? Picking up men in bars...coming as near as dammit to selling herself to them—if not for money then certainly for the pseudo-love they had offered her.

It wasn't her fault, his heart had protested in loving defence. She had been deprived of her father's love as a child. She was simply trying to compensate for that. With love, *his* love, she could be made whole again. She would forget her past and so would he. What mattered was the here and now and the future they would share...a future which meant nothing to him without her in it.

And so it had continued, on and on, when he was supposed to be working. In the end he had had no option other than to give in, and now he was on his way to find Saskia to tell her...ask her...to beg her if necessary.

'Is Saskia still outside?' he asked Athena, impatient to tell Saskia how he felt.

Athena's eyes narrowed. She knew that look in a man's eyes, and to see it now, in the eyes of the only man she wanted, was not to be tolerated. If Saskia couldn't be induced to leave Andreas then *he* must reject her, and Athena knew exactly how to make *that* happen.

'Oh...' Immediately she faked a look of concern, 'Didn't you know? She's gone for a walk...with Ari. I know you won't like me saying this, Andreas, but—well, we all know how much Ari likes women, and Saskia *has* been making it rather obvious that she reciprocates... Not whilst you're around, of course...'

'Andreas—' Pia tried to stop him several minutes later but he refused to stop or listen.

'Not now Pia, whatever it is...' he said brusquely, before striding down the corridor towards his suite.

Goodness, but he looked angry, Pia reflected as she watched his departing back. Well, what she had to tell him wasn't going to lighten his bad mood, but he would have to be told. She knew that.

Andreas could hear the sound of the shower running as he walked into the bedroom and slammed the door behind him.

'Saskia?' he demanded, striding towards the bathroom and pulling open the door.

Saskia blanched as she saw him. She had just that second stepped out of the shower and wrapped a towel around her damp body—thank goodness.

'Why are you having a shower?' Andreas demanded suspiciously.

Saskia stared at him nonplussed.

'I've just been for a walk and it was hot and...'

Andreas could feel the shock of his jealously jolt right through his body, exploding inside him, almost a physical pain. It furnished him with some very vivid and very sexual images of just why Saskia might want to cool down. Like any man in love, he couldn't bear the thought of his beloved in the arms of someone else, and he reacted predictably.

Taking hold of her, his fingers gripping painfully into the delicate flesh of her upper arms, he gritted jealously, 'You just couldn't wait, could you? Where did he take you?'

'He...?' Saskia started to protest, confused by both his words and his actions. 'What on earth...?'

But Andreas wasn't listening.

'Was it out in the open, where anyone could have seen you? Is *that* what you like, Saskia...demeaning yourself so completely that...? But of course you do. I already know that, don't I? You *want* to be treated badly, to be used and then discarded like a... Well, then, if that's the way you like it then let's see if *I* can come up to your expectations, shall we? If I can give you what you so obviously want.'

He was a man no longer in control of what he was doing, wanting passionately to stamp his possession on her—body and soul—to make her his and wipe from her memory all thoughts of any other man!

What on earth had happened to turn Andreas from the cool, remote man she was familiar with into the raw explosion of male fury and passion she was facing now? Saskia wondered in bemusement. It was passion she could sense most strongly, she recognised dizzily. It emanated from him like a heat haze, drawing her into its danger and excitement, melting, burning away her own protective caution.

Wasn't this secretly what a part of her had *wanted* to happen? For him to look at her as he was doing now, with the fierce, elemental need of a man no longer able to fight off his own desire.

Somehow, seeing Andreas so close to losing control allowed her to give full reign to her own feelings and longings.

'You're mine,' Andreas was telling her rawly as he pulled her hard against his body. 'Mine, Saskia… And what is mine I mean to have full measure of,' he added thickly.

Saskia could feel her skin starting to quiver responsively where he was touching it. He slid his hands oh, so deliberately up her bare arm and over her shoulder, his fingertips caressing the nape of her neck. Blissfully she arched her spine, offering herself up to his touch, feeling the quiver-raising goosebumps on her skin moving deeper, growing stronger, as they became a pulse that echoed and then drove her heartbeat.

'Kiss me, Andreas…'

Had she actually said that? Demanded it in that

unfamiliar husky little voice that sounded so sexy and made Andreas's eyes glitter even more hotly?

'Oh, I can promise you that I'm going to do far more than just kiss you,' Andreas assured her as his hands very deliberately removed the towel from her body. 'Far, far more,' he repeated sensually, before adding, 'But if a kiss is what you want...'

His hands were spread against her collarbone and her throat, his thumbs massaging her fragile bones, his lips brushing just the merest tantalising breath of heat against the pulse that raced so frantically beneath her skin.

'Where exactly is it you want me to kiss you, Saskia?' he was asking her. 'Here...? Here...? Here..?'

As his mouth moved tantalisingly over her throat and then her jaw, covering every inch of her face but her lips, Saskia heard herself start to moan softly with longing until, unable to endure any more of his delicious torment, she put her hand against his face and turned his mouth to hers, exhaling in a soft swoon of relief as she finally tasted the hard warmth she had been aching for.

'Andreas... Andreas...' She could hear herself whispering his name as she slid her fingers into his hair and clasped his head, probing the hard outline of his lips with small, frantic thrusts of her tongue-tip.

Over her shoulder Andreas caught sight of their entwined reflections in the mirror. Saskia's naked back view was as perfectly sculpted as that of any classical statue, but her body was composed of living, breathing flesh, and just the feel of her sweetly firm breasts pressing against him, never mind what the dedicated assault of her honey tongue was doing to him, totally obliterated everything but the way he felt about her.

Against the delicate pallor of her Celtic skin his hands looked shockingly male and dark as he caressed her, held her, moulded her so close to his body that he could taste her small gasp of sensual pleasure as she felt his arousal. His clothes were a hindrance he no longer wanted, but he couldn't make the time to remove them until he had punished that sexily tormenting tongue of hers for the way it was destroying his self-control.

He felt the deep, racking shudder of pleasure that ran right through her body as he opened his mouth on hers, taking into his domain full control of their kiss and of her.

Saskia gasped and trembled, yielding the sweet intimacy of her mouth and the soft-fleshed nakedness of her body to Andreas's dominance. What was happening between them was surely the pinnacle of her whole life, the reason she had been born. Here, in Andreas's arms, love and desire were coming together for her in the most perfect way possible.

Saskia had forgotten what she had been going to tell him, why it was so imperative for her to leave. *This* was what she had wanted to happen from the very first second she had set eyes on him.

Unable to bring himself to break the intoxicating sensuality of their shared kiss, Andreas picked Saskia up and carried her over to the bed. Whatever she had been before no longer mattered. From now on she would be his.

The heavy natural linen curtains Saskia had closed over the large windows before taking her shower diffused the strong sunlight outside, bathing the room in a softly muted glow that turned her fair skin almost ethereally translucent. As he laid her on the bed Andreas gave in to the temptation to caress the taut quivering peak of one breast with his lips, savouring it in a slow, careful exploration which made Saskia's whole body shake with sharply intense arousal.

'No, I don't want to rush this,' Andreas denied to her, his voice thick, almost cracking over the words as he refused the frantic pleas of her writhing body. 'I want to take my time and savour everything!' he emphasised as his hand caressed the breast he had just been suckling, his thumb tip etching unbearably erotic circles around the sensitively receptive nub of flesh.

'I want you so much,' Saskia whispered achingly. 'I want you...' She stopped, her eyes clouding with a mixture of anxiety and uncertainty as she heard her own voice and briefly recognised her own danger.

It was too late. Andreas had heard her. Pausing in the act of removing his clothes, he leaned over her, bracing himself so that the muscles in his arms corded tautly, capturing her awed gaze whilst he asked her rawly, 'Where do you want me, Saskia? Tell me... Show me...'

But he already knew the answer to his question because he had already lifted his hand from the bed and brushed his knuckles in the gentlest of touches the full length of the centre of her body, letting it come to rest palm-down against the soft swelling of her most intimate heart.

'You haven't answered my question, Saskia,' he reminded her softly, as his fingertips drew delicate circles of pleasure against her, so jaw-clenching desirable that Saskia thought she might actually faint from the heat and intensity of the longing they were arousing.

'Tell me...tell me what you want,' Andreas was insisting, spacing each word between kisses so ravishingly tender that Saskia felt as though she was melting.

In the cocoon of her own private world he had become for Saskia the lodestone that drew her, the focus of everything she was experiencing, of everything she was and ever wanted to be, the centre of her world.

'I want you,' she responded feverishly to him. 'I want you, Andreas. I...' She shuddered, unable to say any more because Andreas was kissing her, sealing her mouth with a kiss that was a hot, passionate brand of possession. As he wrapped his arms around her Saskia clung to him shyly, stroking the side of his face.

'Look at me,' he demanded.

Hesitatingly she did so, the melting, soft, languorous longing of her gaze entrapped by the hot, fierce glitter of his.

Very slowly and tenderly he began to caress her. Saskia felt as though her whole body was going to dissolve with her longing for him, her need of him.

She reached out to touch his bare shoulder, his arm, and made a helpless little sound of taut female need against his throat as she pressed her lips to it.

Beneath his hands her body softened and responded magically, welcomingly, as though his touch was a special key. But *he* was the key to what she was feeling, Saskia acknowledged hazily, lost fathoms—oceans—deep in her love for him.

'There isn't going to be much time...I want you too much,' he told her almost bluntly, softening the words with another hotly passionate kiss that made her hips lift achingly against him whilst her whole body writhed in longing for him.

'Next time we can take things more slowly,' Andreas gasped harshly against her breast, his voice and actions revealing his increasing need.

Next time... Saskia felt as though she might die from happiness. 'Next time' meant that he shared her feelings, that he felt the same way as she did.

It seemed to Saskia almost as though the air between them throbbed with the intensity of their shared passion, with the way their bodies synchronised together with a perfection surely only given to true lovers.

Each sigh, each gasp, each heartbeat served only to bind her closer to him, emotionally as well as physically, until she was captive to him and her desire, her love, was laid as bare to him as her quivering body.

When he finally whispered to her, 'Now, Saskia... Oh, God, now!' she knew her body had given him its most eager assent before her lips could even begin to frame the words she wanted to say. Automatically she was already wrapping the slim length of her legs around his waist, raising up to meet him, to feel him. She heard him cry out as he entered her, a sound of both torment and triumph, and then he was filling her with his own unique intimate, heavy warmth, and her body, pausing only to tense briefly in sweetly virginal shock, welcomed each ever deepening thrust of him within her.

Andreas felt her body's unexpected resistance, his brain and his emotions even registered their shock at what it meant, but his body refused to react to that knowledge. It loved the hot snug fit of her around him, holding and caressing him, urging him to forget what he had just experienced and to satisfy the age-old demand her femaleness was making on his male-ness. Deeper, harder, stronger, until you reach the deepest heart of me, each delicately soft contraction of her flesh around his urged him. Deeper, stronger, surer, until you are *there*. Yes, there...*there*...

Andreas felt as though his heart and lungs might burst as he drove them both to the place where they could finally fly free.

Saskia cried out in softly sweet awe and relish as she experienced for herself what true completion was...what it truly meant to be a woman, completely fulfilled, elevated to a place, a state...an emotion so piercingly intense that it filled her eyes with hot, happy exhausted tears.

Someone was trembling... Was it her...or was it both of them? She had heard Andreas groan in those final unbelievable seconds before he had wrapped his arms securely around her and then sent them both hurtling into infinity, calling out her name in a way that had made her tingle with raw emotion.

As he fought to regain control of his breathing, and himself, Andreas looked down at Saskia.

She was crying, huge silent tears. Of pain? Because of *him*...because he had...?

Even now his thoughts skidded away from the reality, the truth that his brain was trying to impose on him. She couldn't have been a virgin... It was impossible.

But his self-anger and guilt told him that it wasn't, and she had been. Unforgivably, he had hurt her and made her cry, selfishly taking his pleasure from her at the price of her innocence, so unable to control what he felt for her that he had not been able to stop when he knew that he should have done.

Sickened by his own behaviour, he pulled away from her.

'Andreas...' Saskia reached out towards him uncertainly. Why was he withdrawing from her? Why wasn't he holding her, caressing her...*loving* and reassuring her?

'What is it...what is wrong?' she begged him.

'Do you really need to ask?' Andreas responded tersely. 'Why didn't you tell me...*stop* me...?'

The anger in his voice was driving away the sweet mist of her joy and replacing it with anxiety and despair. It was obvious to her now that what had been so wonderful, so perfect, so *unique* for her had been nowhere near the same kind of experience for Andreas.

Andreas was furious with himself for not somehow having had the insight to know. She had been a virgin, and he, damn him, had practically forced himself on her... He was disgusted with himself, his pride scorched not just by his actions but his complete misreading of her.

'You *should* have stopped me,' he repeated as he got off the bed and went into the bathroom, returning with a towel wrapped around his naked body and his robe, which he handed to Saskia, and sitting down on the bed, turning away from her as she tried to put it on.

What would he say if she were to tell him that the last thing she had wanted was for him to stop? Saskia wondered wretchedly. Her hands were shaking so much she could hardly pull the robe on, never mind fasten it, and when Andreas turned to look at her he gave an impatient, irritated sigh and pushed her hands out of the way, pulling it on properly for her.

'You aren't safe to be let out alone. You realise that, don't you?' he exploded savagely. 'Even if *I* hadn't, Aristotle—'

'Aristotle!' Saskia picked his name up with loathing in her voice and in her eyes. She shuddered, and told him fiercely, 'No—never... He's loathsome and...'

'But you went for a walk with him...'

'No, I didn't,' Saskia protested.

'Athena said you'd gone for a walk,' Andreas insisted, but Saskia wouldn't let him finish.

'Yes, I did...on my own. There were things I wanted...' She stopped, lowering her head and looking away from him. Then she told him in a tear-filled voice, 'I want to go home, Andreas. I can't...'

He knew what she was saying; of course he did, Andreas acknowledged—and why! Of *course* she wanted to get away from him after what he had done...the way he had...

'You should have told me.' He stopped her sharply. 'If I'd known that you were a virgin...'

He might be concerned about taking her virginity but he obviously had no compunction at all about breaking her heart, Saskia decided angrily. For her the loss of her emotional virginity was something that hurt far more—and would continue to hurt.

How could she have been stupid enough to think he felt the same way about her as she did about him? She must have been crazy...*had* been crazy, she recognised grimly. Crazy with love for him!

'I thought...' she heard him saying, but now it was her turn not to allow him to finish.

'I know what you thought,' she cut in with sharp asperity. 'You've already made it very plain *what* you thought of me, Andreas. You thought I was some cheap, silly woman throwing herself at you because of your money. And when I tried to explain you wouldn't let me. You *wanted* to believe the worst of me. I suppose that Greek male pride of yours wouldn't allow you to acknowledge that you might just possibly be wrong...'

Andreas looked at her. His jealousy had led to this...had led to his unforgivably appalling treatment of her. He ached to be able to take her in his arms, to kiss away the traces of tears still on her face, to hold her and whisper to her how much he loved her, how much he wanted to protect her and care for her...how much he wished he could wipe away the wrong he had done her, the pain he had caused her... He ached too, if he was honest, to lie her down on the bed beside him, to remove the robe she was wearing and to kiss every silky inch of her adorable body, to tell her how he felt about her, to show her too. But of course he could do no such thing...not now...

To keep his mind off what he was feeling...off the way he wanted her, he told her gruffly, 'Explain to me now.'

For a moment Saskia was tempted to refuse, but what was the point? She *would* tell him, and then she would tell him that she intended to leave—but she certainly wouldn't tell him why.

Just for an irrational silly female heartbeat of time she ached for him to reach for her, to stop hurting her with words she did not want to hear and to caress and kiss her until her poor deluded heart believed once again that he loved her as she did him.

But thankfully she had enough instinct for self-preservation left to stop herself from telling him so. Instead she began to explain about Megan and Mark and Lorraine.

'She made you do *what*?' Andreas demanded angrily.

She was hesitantly explaining about Lorraine, and her insistence that Saskia make herself look more sexy, when, after a brief rap on the door, Pia burst in and told them, 'Grandfather has arrived. He wants to see both of you.'

'I'd better get dressed,' Saskia mumbled self-consciously.

Pia seemed oblivious to her embarrassment, adding urgently, 'Oh, and Andreas, there's something I want to talk to you about...before you see Grandfather.'

'If you're going to ask for an advance on your

allowance,' Saskia heard Andreas saying hardily to Pia as he walked with her to the door, allowing Saskia to make her own escape to the bathroom, 'you haven't picked a very good time.'

CHAPTER TEN

SASKIA glared reprovingly at the reflection glowing back at her from the bedroom mirror. Her own reflection. The reflection of a woman whose body had enjoyed in full measure every nuance of sensual satisfaction and was proud to proclaim that fact to the world.

That was *not* how she wanted to look when she confronted Andreas's grandfather—the man who was ultimately responsible for her being here...the man who did not think she was good enough for his grandson...the man who preferred to see him marry Athena. Neither did she want *Andreas* to see her like this.

Why on earth couldn't her idiotic body see beyond the delicious fulfilment it was currently basking in and instead think ahead to the loneliness and pain her emotions already knew were lying in store?

Andreas had returned to their room very briefly after Pia's interruption, showering and dressing quickly and then informing her that, although his grandfather was insisting that he wanted to meet her as soon as possible, there were certain matters he needed to discuss with him in private first.

'It won't take very long,' he had told her grimly, before striding out of the room without giving her a chance to tell him that right now, for her own sanity and safety, she wanted to get as far away from him as fast as she could.

Soon, now, he would be coming back for her, to take her and introduce her formally to his grandfather.

Saskia pulled an angry face at her still glowing reflection. She looked, she admitted angrily, the perfect picture of a woman in love. Even her eyes had a new sparkle, a certain glint that said she was hugging to herself a wonderful, special secret.

She had tried over and over again to tell her love-crazed body just what the real situation was, but it simply refused to listen. And so now... She gave a nervous start as she heard the bedroom door opening...

Andreas took a deep breath before reaching out for the bedroom door handle and grasping it firmly.

Pia had been so incensed, so protective and angry on Saskia's behalf, that it had taken her several minutes to become calm enough to spill out in a way that made sense the conversation she had overheard between Athena and Saskia.

'Athena actually tried to bribe Saskia to leave you. She promised her a million pounds if she did. Of course Saskia refused, but I don't see why Athena should be allowed to get away with such insulting and...and offensive behaviour. Grandfather should be told what she's really like—and if you aren't prepared to tell him...' she had threatened darkly.

'Andreas?' she had demanded when he made no response, obviously puzzled at his lack of reaction, but Andreas had still been trying to come to terms with the 'insulting' and 'offensive' behaviour *he* had already inflicted on Saskia. Now, to learn what Athena had done and how nobly Saskia had behaved made him feel... How *could* he have been so wrong about her, so judgemental and...and biased?

A tiny inner voice told him that he already knew the answer. Right from the first second he had set eyes on her there had been something—a sharp warning thrill of sensation and, even more dangerously, of emotion—which he had instantly tried to suppress. His infernal pride had resented the fact that he could fall in love with a woman who was so obvious, and because he had listened to his pride, and not his heart, he had witlessly destroyed something that could have been the most wonderful, the most *precious* part of his life. Unless... Unless Saskia could be persuaded to give him a second chance...

But, whether or not she would allow him the chance to prove his love for her, there was something that *had* to be done, a reparation that *had* to be made. He was Greek enough to think that Saskia should bear his name well before there was any chance of the world knowing that she might bear his child. She had given him her innocence and in exchange he would give her his protection, whether or not she wanted it.

He had told his grandfather exactly what he planned to do, adding truthfully that Saskia was far more important to him than wealth and position and even the love and respect of his grandfather himself.

He had even been tempted to refuse to allow his grandfather to meet her, rather than subject Saskia to any possible hurt or upset, but there was no way he wanted his grandfather to think that he was hiding Saskia from him because he feared she would not be good enough for him. Not good enough! She was *too* good, *too* wonderful...*too* precious...

His final act before heading back to the bedroom had been to tell Athena to leave the island immediately.

'Don't bother to try and persuade my grandfather to allow you to stay. He won't,' he had warned her truthfully.

Now he hesitated before going into the bedroom. He could see Saskia standing waiting for him, and his heart rocked on a huge surge of longing and love for her.

She looked as radiant as a bride, her eyes sparkling, her mouth curved in a smile that was a cross between pure joy and a certain secret, newly discovered womanliness. She looked...

She looked like a woman who had just left the arms and the bed of the man she loved.

But the moment she saw him her expression changed; her eyes became shadowed, her body tense and wary.

Helplessly Andreas closed his eyes, swamped by a wave of love and guilt. He longed more than anything right now to close the door on the rest of the world, to take her in his arms and hold her there for ever whilst he begged for her forgiveness and for the opportunity to spend the rest of his life showing her how much he loved her.

But he had his responsibilities, and primarily, right now, he had to fulfil the promise he had just made to his grandfather that he would introduce Saskia to him.

For his grandfather's sake he trusted that the older man would remember the promise *he* had made that he would treat Saskia gently.

As Andreas crossed the room and took hold of her

hand Saskia shrank back from him, terrified of betraying her feelings, knowing that she was trembling
from head to foot simply because of the warmth of
his hand clasping hers.

She knew that he was bound to make some irritated, impatient comment about the role she was supposed to be playing, but instead he simply released
her hand and told her in a low voice, 'I'm sorry to
have put you through this my…Saskia…'

'It's what you brought me here for,' Saskia reminded him brutally, not daring to look at him.
Surely she must be imagining that raw note of remorse in his voice.

As they left the room the pretty little maid who
looked after it came in, and Andreas paused to say
something to her in Greek before following Saskia
into the corridor.

It was only natural in the circumstances, Saskia
knew, that Andreas should take hold of her hand
again and close the distance between them, so that
when they walked into the cool, simply furnished
room that gave out onto the main patio area they did
so with every outward appearance of a couple deeply
in love. But what was surely less natural, and almost
certainly unwise, was the sense of warmth and security that she got from being so close to him.

To try and distract herself from the effect
Andreas's proximity was having on her, Saskia
looked to where his sister and mother were standing
talking to an elderly white-haired man Saskia knew
must be Andreas's grandfather.

As they walked towards him he started to turn
round, and Saskia could hear Andreas saying for-

mally, 'Grandfather, I'd like to introduce Saskia to you.'

But Saskia had stopped listening, her attention focused instead on the familiar features of the man now facing her. He was the same man she had seen in the street in Athens, the man who had seemed so unwell and whom she had been so concerned about. He didn't look ill now though. He was smiling broadly at them both, coming forward to clasp Saskia's free hand in both of his in a grip heart-rockingly similar to that of his grandson.

'There is no need to introduce her to me, 'Reas.' He laughed. 'Your beautiful fiancée and I have already met.'

Saskia could see how much he was enjoying the shocking effect of his announcement on his family. He was obviously a man who liked to feel he was in control of things...people...who liked to challenge and surprise them. But where that trait in Andreas had angered her, in his grandfather she found it almost endearing.

'You and Saskia have already met?' Andreas was repeating, frowning heavily as he looked from his grandfather to Saskia.

'Yes. In Athens,' his grandfather confirmed before Saskia could say anything. 'She was very kind to an old man, and very concerned for him too. My driver told me that you had expressed your concern for my health to him,' he told Saskia in a broadly smiling aside. 'And I have to confess I did find that walk in the heat plus the wait I had for you to return from the Acropolis a trifle...uncomfortable. But not, I suspect, as uncomfortable as Andreas was, arriving at my office to discover that I had cancelled our meeting,' he added with a chuckle.

'You didn't really think I'd allow my only grandson to marry a woman I knew nothing about, did you?' he asked Andreas with a little swagger that made her hide a small smile. He was so very Greek, so very macho. She knew she should be annoyed, but he was so pleased with himself that she didn't have the heart to be cross.

Andreas, though, as it soon became obvious, was not so easily appeased.

'You decided to check up on Saskia—?' he thundered, giving his grandfather a hard look.

'You have definitely made a good choice, Andreas,' his grandfather interrupted him. 'She is charming…and kind. Not many young women would have taken the time to look after an old man who was a stranger to them. I had to meet her for myself, Andreas. I know you, and—'

'What you have done is an insult to her,' Andreas cut him off coldly, whilst Saskia stared at him in astonishment. Andreas defending and protecting *her*? What was this? And then, abruptly, she remembered that he was simply acting out a role…the role of a loving protective fiancé.

'And let me tell you this, Grandfather,' Andreas was continuing. 'Whether you approve of Saskia or not makes no difference to me. I *love* her, and I always will, and there are no threats, no bribes, no blandishments you can offer that could in any way change that.'

There was a brief pause before the older man nodded his head.

'Good,' he announced. 'I'm glad to hear it. A woman like Saskia deserves to be the focus of her husband's heart and life. She reminds me very much of my Elisabeth,' he added, his eyes suddenly misty. 'She had that same kindness, that same concern for others.' Suddenly he started to frown as he caught sight of Saskia's ring.

'What is *that* she is wearing?' he demanded. 'It is not fit for a Demetrios bride. I'm surprised at you, Andreas…a paltry plain solitaire. She shall have my Elisabeth's ring, and—'

'No.' The harshness in Andreas's voice made Saskia tense. Was he going to tell his grandfather that it was all a lie? Was the thought of Saskia wearing something as sacred to their family as his dead grandmother's ring too much for him to endure?

'No,' he continued. 'If Saskia wants a different ring then she shall choose one herself. For now I want her to wear the one *I* chose for her. A diamond as pure and shiningly beautiful as she is herself.'

Saskia could see Andreas's mother's and sister's jaws dropping, as was her own at such an unexpectedly tender and almost poetic declaration.

Ridiculously tears blurred her eyes as she looked down at the solitaire. It *was* beautiful. She thought so every time she put it on. But for her to treasure such a ring it would have to be given with love. It was the commitment it was given with that made it of such value to a woman in love, not its financial worth.

But Andreas's grandfather was brushing aside such irrelevancies, and demanding jovially, 'Very well, but what I want to know now is when you plan to get married. I can't live for ever, Andreas, and if I am to see your sons…'

'Grandfather…' Andreas began warningly.

Later, after a celebratory lunch and rather more vintage champagne than had perhaps been wise, Saskia made her way with solemn concentration back to her room. Andreas was with her, as befitted a loving and protective fiancé.

Outside the room Andreas touched her lightly on her arm, so that she was forced to stop and look at him.

'I'm sorry about what happened in Athens,' he told her, his brusqueness giving way to anger as he added, 'My grandfather had no right to subject you to—'

'In his shoes you would have done exactly the same thing,' Saskia interrupted him quietly, immediately leaping to his grandfather's defence. 'It's a perfectly natural reaction. I can remember still the way my grandmother reacted the first time I went out on a date.' She laughed, and then stopped as she saw that Andreas was shaking his head.

'Of course she would be protective of you,' he agreed flatly. 'But didn't my grandfather realise the danger you could have been in? What if he had mistimed his ''accidental'' meeting with you? You were alone in an unfamiliar city. He had countermanded my instructions to your driver by telling him to keep out of sight until he saw him return to his own car.'

'It was broad daylight, Andreas,' Saskia pointed out calmly. But she could see that Andreas wasn't going to be appeased. 'Well, at least your grandfather won't be trying to convince you that you should marry Athena anymore,' she offered placatingly as they walked into the bedroom. She came to an abrupt halt as she saw the new cases Andreas had bought her for their trip in the middle of the bedroom floor. 'What...?' she began unsteadily but Andreas didn't let her finish.

'I told Maria to pack for both of us. We're booked onto the first flight in the morning for Heathrow.'

'We're leaving?'

Even as she spoke Saskia knew that showing her shock was a giveaway piece of folly. Of course they were leaving. After all, there was no need for Andreas to keep her here any more. His grandfather had made it very plain during lunch that Athena would no longer be welcome beneath his roof.

'We don't have any option,' Andreas replied flatly. 'You heard my grandfather. Now that he's been given a clean bill of health he's itching to find something to occupy him. Organising our wedding and turning it into something between a lavish extravaganza worthy of a glossy magazine and a chance to gather as many of his business cronies under one roof as he can isn't going to be an opportunity he'll want to miss out on. And my mother and sister will be just as bad.' He started to scowl. 'Designer outfits, a wedding dress that could take months to make, plans to extend the villa so that it can accommodate the children my mother and my grandfather are so determined we're going to have...'

Greedily Saskia drank in every word. The mental image he was creating for her, the blissful pictures he was painting were becoming more alluring with every word he said. Mistily she allowed herself to dream about what she knew to be impossible—and then Andreas's next words sent her into shocked freefall.

'We need to get married immediately. We just don't have the time for that kind of delay. Not after... If you are already carrying my child then...'

'What are you saying?' Saskia protested, white-faced. 'You can't be serious. We *can't* get married just because...'

'Just because what?' Andreas challenged her bitterly. 'Because you were a virgin, an innocent who had never known a man before? I...I am Greek, Saskia, and there is no way I would *ever* abandon any child I had fathered. Under the circumstances there is nothing else we *can* do.'

'You're only half-Greek,' Saskia heard herself reminding him dizzily, before adding, 'And anyway I may not even be pregnant. In fact I'm sure I'm not.'

Andreas gave her a dry, almost withering look.

'And you're an expert on such things, of course. You, a woman who hasn't even...'

'They say you don't always...not the first time...' Saskia told him lamely, but she could see from his face that he had as little faith in that particular old wives' tale as she did herself.

'I don't want this, Andreas,' she insisted, trying another tack. Her voice and her body had both begun to shake with shock at what Andreas intended.

'Even if I am to...to have a child...these days that doesn't mean... I could bring it up by myself...'

'What on?' he challenged her. 'Not the one million pounds you turned down from Athena, obviously.'

Saskia's eyes looked bewildered at the way he'd slipped the thrust up under her guard.

'A child needs more than money. Much, much more,' she defended herself quickly. How did he know about Athena's offer to her? Athena herself wouldn't have told him. 'A child needs love,' she continued.

'Do you think *I* don't know that?' Andreas shot back. 'After all, surely I am far better placed to know it than you, Saskia. I had the love of both my parents as a child, and I can promise you I would *never* allow a child of mine to grow up without my love.'

He stopped abruptly as he heard the quick indrawn gasp of pain she had given, his eyes darkening with remorse.

'Saskia, my beloved heart, I am so sorry. I didn't mean to hurt you, just to make you understand that I could no more walk away from our child than I can from you.'

Saskia stared at him, unable to speak, to move, to breathe as she listened to the raw fervency of his declaration. He was acting. He had to be. He *didn't* love her. She *knew* that. And somehow hearing him say to her the words she so much ached to hear whilst knowing they were lies filled her with more anguish than she could bear.

Tugging frantically at the ring he had given her, she started to pull it off, her eyes dark with anger, sparkling with tears of pride and pain whilst Andreas watched her as he had been watching her all through lunch, and then afterwards when the wine she had drunk had relaxed her.

'I felt so angry when Athena offered Saskia that money,' Pia had told him passionately. 'And so proud of her. She loves you so much. I used to think that no one could ever be good enough for you, my wonderful brother, but now I know I was wrong. She loves you every bit as much as you deserve to be loved, as I one day want to love the man I marry...'

'She is perfect for you, darling,' his mother had whispered to him.

'She is a beautiful young woman with an even more beautiful heart,' his grandfather had said emotionally.

There had been one unguarded moment after lunch, when his grandfather had been teasing her about something and she had turned to him, as though seeking his protection. The look in her eyes had made him ache to snatch her up and carry her away somewhere he could have her all to himself and create that look over and over again.

Finally she managed to pull the ring off, holding it out to him she told him, head held high, 'There is no way I would ever marry a man who does not love me.'

Andreas closed his eyes, replayed the words to make sure he hadn't misheard them, and then opened his eyes again and walked purposefully towards her. He was about to take the biggest gamble he had ever taken in his entire life. If he lost he would lose everything. If he won...

He took a deep breath and asked Saskia softly, 'Shouldn't that be you wouldn't ever marry a man you did not love?'

Saskia froze, her face going white and then a soft, deepening shade of pink.

'I...that was what I meant,' she began, and then stopped as panic overwhelmed her. 'I can't marry you, Andreas,' she protested as he closed the distance between them, masterfully sweeping her up into his arms.

'And I won't let you go, Saskia,' he told her in a low, throbbing voice.

'Because of what happened…because there might be a baby?' she guessed, but the words had to be mumbled because Andreas was holding her so tightly, his lips brushing irresistibly tender kisses against her throat and then her jaw, moving closer and closer to her mouth.

'Because of that,' he agreed, whispering the words against her lips. 'And this…and you…'

'Me?' Saskia started to squeak, but Andreas wouldn't let her.

Cupping her face instead, he looked down into her eyes, his own grave with pain, heavy with remorse, hot with love and desire, as he begged her, 'Please give me a chance to show you how things could be between us, Saskia. To show you how good it could be, how good it *will* be…'

'What are you trying to say?' Saskia demanded dizzily.

Still cupping her face, Andreas told her, 'I'm trying to say with words what my emotions, my heart, my soul and my body have already told you, my beloved heart, my adored, precious love. Surely you must have guessed, felt how it was for me when we made love?'

Lifting her head so that she could look into his eyes, search them to see if she actually dared believe what she was hearing, Saskia felt her heart starting to thud in a heady mixture of joy and excitement. No man could possibly fake the way Andreas was looking at her, and if that wasn't enough his body was giving her a very distinct and intimate message of its own. Unable to help herself Saskia started to blush a little as she felt her own body respond to Andreas's arousal.

'I...I thought that must just be sex,' she told him bravely.

'What have I said?' she demanded in bewilderment when Andreas started to laugh.

'My dearest love,' he told her, still laughing, 'if I hadn't already had incontrovertible proof of your innocence, that remark would have furnished me with it. *Any* woman who had experienced "just sex" would have known immediately that—' He stopped and smiled down at her, tenderly kissing her before telling her gruffly.

'No. Why should I bother to explain? After all, there's never going to be any way that you will know what it is to have "just sex". You and I, Saskia, will be making love, sharing love, giving one another love for all our lives.'

'Oh, Andreas,' Saskia whispered deliriously as he pulled her firmly into his arms.

'No, Andreas, we can't,' she protested five minutes later as he carried her towards the bed and started to undress her.

'All my clean clothes are packed...I won't have anything to wear...and...'

'Good,' Andreas informed her without the remotest hint of remorse. 'I can't think of anything I want more right now than to have you naked in my bed with no means of escape.'

'Mmm... That's funny,' Saskia told him impishly. 'I was thinking exactly the same thing myself!'

EPILOGUE

'WELL, your grandfather may not have got his own way over our wedding, but he certainly wasn't going to allow us to have a quiet family christening!' Saskia laughed with Andreas as they both surveyed the huge crowd of people filling the recently completed and refurbished 'special occasions' suite at the group's flagship British hotel.

'Mmm… Are you sure that Robert will be okay with him?' Andreas asked anxiously as he focused with fatherly concern on the other side of the room, where his grandfather was proudly showing off his three-month-old great-grandson to his friends and business cronies.

'Well, as your grandfather keeps on reminding us, he's held far more babies than you or I in his time,' Saskia said, laughing.

'Maybe, but none of them has been *our* son,' Andreas returned promptly, adding, 'I think I'd better go and retrieve him, Sas. He looks as though he might be starting to get fretful, and he never finished that last feed…'

'Talk about doting fathers,' Pia murmured to Saskia as they both watched Andreas hurrying proprietorially towards his son. 'I always knew that Andreas would be a good father, mind you…'

Saskia smiled at her as she watched her husband expertly holding their son—born nine months and one day exactly after their quiet wedding, tactfully arriving three weeks after his predicted birth date. But of course only she and Andreas knew *that*...just as only they knew as yet that by the time he reached his first birthday he would have a brother or a sister.

'Isn't that a bit too soon?' Andreas had protested when she had first told him her suspicions, and Saskia had blushed and then laughed, remembering, as she was sure Andreas was as well, that *she* had been the one to initiate their first lovemaking after Robert's birth.

Andreas was the most wonderful father, and an even more wonderful husband and lover. Saskia gave a small sigh, a look darkening her eyes that Andreas immediately recognised.

If his mother was surprised to be suddenly handed her grandson whilst Andreas insisted that there was something he needed to discuss with his wife in private, she gave no sign of it, going instead to join Saskia's grandmother, with whom she had already formed a close bond.

'Andreas! No, we *can't*,' Saskia protested as Andreas led her to the most luxurious of the hotel's refurbished bedrooms and locked the door.

'Why not?' he teased her. 'We own the hotel and we are married—and right now I want you so much.'

'Mmm... Andreas...' Saskia sighed as his lips found the exquisitely tender cord in her throat that always and unfailingly responded to the sweet torment of his lips.

'Mmm... Andreas...what?' he mouthed against her skin.

But Saskia didn't make any verbal response, instead pulling his head down towards her own, her mouth opening sweetly beneath his.

'I knew the first moment I set eyes on you that you were a wanton woman.' Andreas laughed tenderly. '*My* wanton woman...'

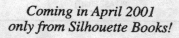

If you enjoyed what you just read,
then we've got an offer you can't resist!

Take 2 bestselling love stories FREE!
Plus get a FREE surprise gift!

LONG, TALL TEXANS

EMMETT, REGAN & BURKE

New York Times
extended list bestselling author

Diana PALMER

returns to Jacobsville, Texas, in this special
collection featuring rugged heroes, spirited
heroines and passionate love stories told
in her own inimitable way!

Coming in May 2001 only from Silhouette Books!

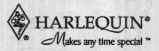

INDULGE IN A QUIET MOMENT
WITH HARLEQUIN

Get a FREE
Quiet Moments Bath Spa

with just two proofs of purchase from any of our four special collector's editions in May.

Harlequin® is sure to make your time special this Mother's Day with four special collector's editions featuring a short story *PLUS* a complete novel packaged together in one volume!

Collection #1 Intrigue abounds in a collection featuring *New York Times* bestselling author Barbara Delinsky and Kelsey Roberts.

Collection #2 Relationships? Weddings? Children? = *New York Times* bestselling author Debbie Macomber and Tara Taylor Quinn at their best!

Collection #3 Escape to the past with *New York Times* bestselling author Heather Graham and Gayle Wilson.

Collection #4 Go West! With *New York Times* bestselling author Joan Johnston and Vicki Lewis Thompson!

Plus Special Consumer Campaign!
Each of these four collector's editions will feature a
"FREE QUIET MOMENTS BATH SPA" offer.
See inside book in May for details.

Only from

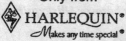

HARLEQUIN®
Makes any time special ®

Don't miss out! Look for this exciting promotion on sale in May 2001, at your favorite retail outlet.

Visit us at www.eHarlequin.com   PHNCP01

Getting down to business in the boardroom... and the bedroom!

A secret romance, a forbidden affair, a thrilling attraction...

What happens when two people work together and simply can't help falling in love—no matter how hard they try to resist?

Find out in our new series of stories set against working backgrounds.

Look out for

THE MISTRESS CONTRACT
by Helen Brooks, Harlequin Presents® #2153
Available January 2001

and don't miss

SEDUCED BY THE BOSS
by Sharon Kendrick, Harlequin Presents® #2173
Available April 2001

Available wherever Harlequin books are sold.

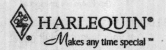

HARLEQUIN®
Makes any time special ™

Visit us at www.eHarlequin.com

HP925